GENERATION

SHADOWS OF THE VOID BOOK 1

J.J. GREEN

INFINITEBOOK

SERIES BOOKS

The Books of Shadows of the Void - Complete Series

Prequel: Starbound
Book 1: Generation
Book 2: Stranded
Book 3: Dawn
Book 4: Shadowrise
Book 5: Underworld
Book 6: Burned
Book 7: Trapped
Book 8: Mars Born
Book 9: Shadow Battle
Book 10: Shadow War
Books 1 - 3 The Galathea Chronicles
Books 4 - 7 The Earth Chronicles
Books 8 - 10 The Galactic Chronicles

1

Jas Harrington snapped her visor in place and took a deep breath of the purified, cooled air that flowed into her combat suit. For the last fifteen minutes she'd been ignoring the prickles that ran down her spine as she prepared her team for the routine LIV—Locate, Investigate, Vacate. But she couldn't ignore the feeling any longer.

"AX7," she said as she entered the shuttle airlock with the fifteen burly, androgynous defense units under her command. The door to the passenger cabin slid closed behind them, and a hiss permeated the enclosed space as the planet's atmosphere entered through newly opened valves, equalizing the air pressure differential.

"C.S.O. Harrington," the unit replied.

"Station yourself at the rear."

"Affirmative, C.S.O. Harrington."

AX7 had been injured in a skirmish with a hostile species a few planets back, and though the unit had self-repaired as programmed, it wasn't factory-perfect like the others were, and those prickles were telling her to expect an attack.

The part-organic, part-robotic Polestar Corp androids shuffled aside in the narrow airlock to allow AX7 through. Jas's excessively long childhood on Mars had resulted in a height of just over two meters, but at two meters thirty the defense units dwarfed her. As usual at close quarters, she was acutely conscious of the difference. The units resembled linebackers padded up, except they had no padding. Thin armored material that was highly resistant to penetration and extreme temperatures coated their large forms.

If the defense units short-circuited and turned on her, well...Jas pushed memories of incidents involving prototypes to the back of her mind. These were the latest, state-of-the-art models, though she wasn't naive enough to imagine Polestar supplied them to protect the crew. No, in the event of an emergency, she was sure the units' first move would be to save precious resource samples.

AX7's face expressed no emotion as it moved to the back of the group, though it had the intellectual capacity to understand why Jas had put it there. Despite her extensive experience working with the units, she hadn't figured out if they genuinely had no feelings at all, or if they weren't able to express them.

"What's the weather like out there, Lingiari?" she asked the shuttle pilot through her radio.

"A little precipitation. Temperature just below zero."

A spark of nostalgia flickered through Jas's sense of foreboding. "Snow? It's snowing?" She hadn't seen snow since attending training college in Antarctica, the last place on Earth it had snowed in twenty years.

"Sure looks like it," the pilot replied.

Jas's brief moment of pleasure was swamped by the realization that snow meant reduced visibility. The prickles down her spine grew so strong she itched to rub her back, impossible though that was in her suit. "Still no bio readings?"

"Nothing bigger than a rat's dick."

Jas rolled her eyes and thumbed a switch on her weapon, changing the setting to flamethrower. Not many life forms could withstand fire. She didn't instruct her defense units on their weaponry. They would compute the optimum response according to the situation, probably better and faster than her. The smartest command strategy was to leave them the hell alone to do their job, unless she knew something they didn't, but as in most LIV assignments, she was the blind leading the blind.

A light flashed above the airlock's outer door. Ten flashes and it would open. The shuttle computer was simultaneously relaying the countdown to the units electronically, but their eyes were also on the light. Defense unit behavior was disarmingly human at times.

The door opened, and the airlock flooded with light and swirling flakes of snow. Jas's visor instantly dimmed, shadowing her view of the terrain outside. A flat, plain landscape stretched to the horizon, lightly powdered with snow and peppered with tough scrub. Except for the low, dull vegetation, the area seemed empty of life. A dark gray structure made up of overlapping hexagonal boxes two or three meters tall dominated the view, against a pale gray, cloudy sky. It wasn't the most inviting planet Jas had visited.

She gave the order to disembark. Moving as one, the defense units set off down the ramp. She followed and took her place at their side. The one point two Earth gravity made moving a little more effort than usual, but it was manageable. Her boots broke through the thin layer of snow, and the familiar thrill of being the first human being to set foot on a new planet surged through her, despite her trepidation.

"No Class P life forms within one K," came Lingiari's voice through her radio. His close-range scanners were telling him the same as the starship's less sensitive long-distance surveillance equipment had indicated before they set out—nothing to worry about, supposedly. Jas'ss grip tightened on her weapon as she accompanied the units toward the matte gray structure.

"Your scanners are penetrating that rock construction, right?" she asked Lingiari.

"Yeah, as far as I can tell, but they aren't picking up anything. Seems to be empty. But it isn't rock. It's a crystal-metal amalgam. And another material the scanners can't identify."

"Artificial?"

"I think you might be confusing me with a scientist. I'm forwarding the results to the ship."

"Sorry. Thanks for the info," Jas replied. Of course the pilot didn't have the knowledge or authority to interpret the data. What was she thinking? She deliberately tensed and then relaxed her muscles. An officer aboard the *Galathea* would update her on anything they thought important. At that moment, no one was saying anything.

She'd reached a hole in the wall of the structure. The defense units were waiting in formation. The hole was hexagonal, mirroring the shape of the structure's blocks. Inside, all was dark.

"C.S.O. Harrington, permission to enter and search," AX5 said.

"Permission granted. AX12, you too."

The two units stepped over a low wall at the base of the hole and dipped their heads as they went inside. Motionless, the other units waited, snowflakes settling on their wide shoulders. A few minutes later, AX5's calm voice came through Jas's radio. "All clear."

She released the breath she hadn't realized she'd been holding. "Follow on," she instructed the rest.

As Jas went in, her dimmed visor cleared, and a light beamed out from her helmet, slicing through the darkness. She was in an empty room just large enough to hold her and thirteen units comfortably. AX5 and 12 were investigating a neighboring chamber. The floor was the same crystal-metal amalgam as the walls and ceiling, and it sloped gradually downward toward several hexagonal holes at the far end. A few steps inside, and Jas could raise her head.

AX12 and 5 appeared at a hole—or doorway?—on the far side. The place was still and silent. The scanner reports seemed accurate. It looked empty, totally devoid of life or artifacts. She divided the units into groups and sent them to investigate deeper inside, accompanying one of the groups herself.

The next room looked the same as the first. No sign of life nor signs that anything had ever lived there. The only break in the monotonous walls was more holes, leading to identical rooms and heading downward, underground and deeper into the structure. From Jas's position as she peered through a hole, the rooms seemed endless.

An hour passed, then two. Jas and the units penetrated deep into the labyrinthine construction. She had to activate her suit's pathfinder function to avoid getting lost. By the time she surfaced, she'd found nothing different from the empty room at the entrance.

Jas had conducted LIVs on many planets. According to strict regulations, they had to vacate immediately at the first sign of intelligence. If there was no intelligent life, the planet's resources were up for grabs to the first corporation that claimed them.

In Jas's experience the evidence of high-level, sentient species was usually clear. Whatever the form of intelligence, evolution always seemed to favor certain expressions of it: the use of tools, modifying the natural environment, storage of resources, training of offspring, and the systemization of food gathering or production and distribution. On K.67092d, the evidence was not clear. The regular, straight lines of the structure indicated artificial construction, but there seemed to be no other evidence of intelligence. If sentient life forms had built the place, where were they? Why had they left, leaving nothing behind?

Leaving the structure, Jas scanned the surroundings again. It had stopped snowing. Nothing moved except the spiny, spindly, leafless branches of the low shrubs, bending slightly, creaking in the steady wind.

"Preliminary report, Harrington?" Akabe Loba's voice came over her radio.

Jas stiffened. As always, the master of the *Galathea* was pushing her, his eye focused solely on his schedule and bonuses. "Initial LIV not complete, sir."

"But no sign of intelligence?"

"It's hard to tell, sir. The structure's—"

"I can see it through your relay, Harrington. Looks geological to me. And there are no artifacts."

Jas's lips drew into a thin line. She knew what was coming. "Sir, it's a little early to conclude—"

"I'm not asking *you* to conclude anything, C.S.O. Harrington. Is the area secure?"

When she didn't answer immediately, Loba repeated his question, louder.

"No hostile life forms encountered, yet," Jas replied through her teeth. *Damn the misborn.* But what could she say? Prickles down her spine didn't count as a reason to delay resource assessment.

2

Prospecting ships like Polestar Corp's *Galathea* ran to a tight timetable. To provide an acceptable return on the company's investment, the crew had to locate and claim at least ten resource-rich planets uninhabited by intelligent life per mission, on average. After that—or maybe before if they stumbled across a planet loaded with a highly valuable substance such as mythrin, base ingredient of blissful, stupor-inducing mythranil—the crew would start to stack up bonuses. Bonuses were the only thing that made it worth enduring the nearly endless boredom and starvation wages of space prospecting.

The ship's master took the lion's share, of course, and the rest of the crew's dividends were portioned out according to rank. As chief security officer, Jas's rank and dividends were in the middle range. She wouldn't be relaxing in the perfumed seas of Balgamon, as First Mate Haggardy planned to do when that mission was over, but neither would she be handing over every penny she had for the most basic genetic upgrade to her as-yet unconceived child, as one of the maintenance crew had mentioned.

Not that Jas planned on having kids anyway. Her own childhood hadn't exactly endeared her to the concept, and she had an irrational fear that her child might turn out to be someone like Master Akabe Loba, into whose blood-threaded eyes she was currently staring.

"Enough arguing, Harrington. Twelve sites. Twelve LIVs, and you've found nothing but some kind of bushworm, gliding non-venomous spiders, and an ambulatory slime mold. Twelve LIVs that turned up no hostile life forms or territory, and you're *still* not prepared to give the all-clear?"

Loba was leaning across a horizontal screen that projected a spinning hologram of K. 67092d. They were in the mission room, where Jas had been summoned to 'discuss' her delay in clearing the planet for resource assessment with the master and other high-ranking officers. The master's head was thrust into the moving holographic image, and the miniature topography played across his features, lending him an even more than usually crazed effect. His carefully coiffed, white-dyed curls seemed about to uncoil and stand on end.

Jas knew she was fighting a losing battle, but she was going to fight it anyway. She was head of security. The safety of the entire crew was her responsibility, and if she had a hunch something on a planet was dangerous, she was going to damn well act on it. She'd never been wrong before.

"I've already told you my reasons. It makes no sense that we've found no intelligent life. Those structures were built. They aren't geological. The building material is artificial, manufactured. We've found nothing else on the planet like it. Something sentient made those buildings. That's what Haggardy's report says." She turned to the first mate for back up. He was seated at the far end of the table and picking at his nails.

First Mate Haggardy held up his hands. "Now wait a minute, Harrington. I wouldn't go that far. I only said we can't conclude it's natural *or* artificial. That's all." He glanced at the master, who was glaring at him.

Jas cursed under her breath. That wasn't how his findings read, and he knew it. Was he planning on rewriting his conclusions? She suspected Haggardy was as interested in his bonus as Loba was, or he was even more of a wimp than she'd taken him for. He was a scientist. He should know better than to risk everyone's lives on a lack of immediate evidence.

She swung back to Loba. "Just because we can't find what built those structures, that doesn't mean they weren't built. The life forms responsible might be hiding. Maybe because they're afraid, or maybe they're waiting to attack. We can't allow Resource Assess on the surface until we know more. We don't have enough defense units to protect them from a full onslaught."

"You seem to be getting confused, Harrington," said Loba quietly, "with your talk of what *we* can and can't do. I shouldn't have to remind you that *I'm* master of this vessel." His facial muscles were rigid. He stood straight and drew himself up to his full height, which was a head shorter than Jas's.

Her stature had always bothered him, she knew, like it seemed to bother many men. But she couldn't help that any more than she could help doing her kratting job.

"The presence of artificial structures does not prohibit a resource claim under deep space property law," the master continued. "Several precedents have been set where such items were found to be relics of extinct species. Maybe the structures are buildings, but if that's the case it's most likely that whatever created them has long since died out—"

"But the fact—"

"THE FACT remains that if there's no sign of intelligent or hostile life after twelve LIVs, the planet's safe enough to assess for resources. Your refusal to give the all clear is a dereliction of duty, and—"

"Sir," exclaimed Navigator Lee, jumping out of her seat like a jack-in-the-box, "if I could—"

"What?" barked Loba, not taking his eyes off Jas, who held his glare and made a special effort to look down at him.

Lee seemed to momentarily regret her decision to come to Jas's aid, but she soldiered on. "C.S.O. Harrington's service has been exemplary throughout the mission," she said quickly, and didn't stop when Loba opened his mouth to speak, but gathered speed. "She saved many lives when we were attacked on K. 87593g." She ran the numbers together: eightsevenfiveninethree. "The defense units were all in the right place at the right time. If it hadn't been for her command of the evacuation, some of us wouldn't be here right now." She looked pointedly at Haggardy, who gazed into space.

"Your point?" asked Loba.

"I just think, if she's worried about the safety of the planet, we should listen."

"Thank you for your input, navigator," said Loba sarcastically, "but if Harrington's prior performance is under scrutiny, your example hardly helps her, does it? After all, if she was any good at her job, the crew would never have been in any danger in the first place."

Jas ground her jaw. She'd warned him. She'd gone to his cabin and warned Loba that there had been an overnight increase in animal tracks around the assessment site, and that she recommended withdrawing the team until she could investigate. It was a warning he'd conveniently forgotten. She wasn't going to let him forget this one.

Her fist thumped the screen and the hologram of the planet wobbled. The officers at the table jumped in their seats. Haggardy got up and backed away.

"I'm chief security officer, and I'm telling you that planet isn't safe. I can't tell you why, and I can't tell you when or where an attack might come from, but I know it *will* come, and I'm *not* giving the all clear. *You* might like to play fast and loose with the lives of two hundred people for the sake of a fat bonus and a regular supply of mythranil, but I sure as hell don't."

As soon as the words were out of her mouth—before, even—she knew she'd gone too far. As she finished, she drew back from the screen. Everyone was still except Lee, who raised a nervous finger to her lips as her gaze flicked between Loba and Jas.

Without taking his eyes from his security officer, Loba murmured, "Hologram, off." The slowly spinning image disappeared and without its illumination, the room became dim. No one moved a muscle to switch on the lights.

Loba was an addict. The whole crew knew. It was why no one was allowed to disturb him for six hours of the quiet shift, on threat of dismissal. It was why he dyed his hair white, to cover up the tell-tale crimson tinge. It was why he breathed quickly even when not exerting himself. In the silence his quiet panting was plain to hear.

"Your judgment is clearly impaired, C.S.O. Harrington. For your own safety and the safety of this ship's crew, you are confined to your cabin until further notice. Should you leave your cabin without permission, you will be placed in the brig for the remainder of the mission. I'll consider your release if you pass a mental health assessment. Haggardy, accompany her."

The first mate rose to his feet and moved toward the door.

Jas whirled on her heel, her fists clenched at her sides, looking for a single sign of support from the other officers. Officers whose lives she'd protected on every planet they'd visited that mission. None met her gaze but Lee, who only grimaced in sympathy.

Haggardy was at the open door, waiting for her. There was nothing to do but leave. She stomped over and exited without another word to Loba or the rest of them. Haggardy struggled to keep up as she marched through the corridors to her cabin. What did it matter if she couldn't tell them why the planet wasn't safe? Didn't her years of experience count for anything?

But though Jas was furious, a stronger emotion overrode her anger: fear. In her eleven years in the job, she'd never been wrong when it came to sensing danger. And all her alarm bells were ringing.

The first mate was the closest person to take out her frustration on. "Thanks for your support."

"Harrington," replied Haggardy, "your case is weak, and we're on a schedule. And you certainly didn't do yourself any favors back there. You shouldn't have lost your temper like that. Mentioning the master's indulgences? Bad move."

Jas turned to him as they arrived at her cabin. "There's something down there. I know there is," she said quietly.

"Been running the blood yourself?" was his reply as her cabin door closed.

3

——————

Carl Lingiari wished for a storm. A super cell or a tornado, like the ones that swept the western New South Wales plains of his boyhood. Storms he'd grown up learning to dodge while crop dusting the family farm. Oh sure, he'd encountered a few. At the last planet but one—he never could remember those strings of Kepler numbers—the place he'd mentally dubbed Arse End of Hell, there'd been a beauty of a buster to dodge. He grinned as he remembered the RA team's cheer when they made it back to the ship. Though the passenger cabin still smelled faintly of vomit, that had been the kind of ride that made piloting worthwhile.

Not this ferry tripping. He took his feet down from his console and scanned the instrument panel. Descent was going smoothly. All readings were normal. They were nearly there. He thumbed the mic on his headset. "Touchdown in five." The 'five' was drawn out as he fought to stifle a yawn. He thumbed his mic off and put up his feet again. The shuttle could just about fly itself. It *did* fly itself most of the time. He was like a parent holding a toddler's reins: only there to stop the kid from doing something stupid.

One day, Carl would pilot a starship. A starship like the *Galathea*. Massive starjump engines below, Raptor Xs to the rear, control and living quarters long, sleek and neat along the top. A handful of pulse cannons on the off chance they encountered a hostile space-faring life form. It hadn't happened in the history human space travel, but you never knew. *That* was the kind of bird he'd fly.

Carl wouldn't be copilot, understudy, backup-in-case-of-disaster anymore. He wouldn't be stuck doing the school run in a rustbucket while someone else got to commute in the latest model. He stretched his arms wide, put his hands behind his head, and closed his eyes.

In his imagination, he was sitting at the control panel of the *Galathea*. His Polestar Corp uniform was clean, crease-free, and neatly buttoned to the neck. His pilot's hat was on his head, set at just enough of an angle to make him look sneck. Wearing your hat while aboard ship wasn't strictly required according to regulations, but he had the corporation's image to consider.

Yeah, he would fly that bird through space with style.

A tall, shapely female figure appeared in his daydream. She moved to his side in the pilot's seat on the *Galathea's* bridge. Who was this? Could it be C.S.O. Harrington, in her tight-fitting combat suit? And what was she doing? She leaned down to whisper in his ear. She had to tell him something important and personal, something that couldn't wait. As she leaned toward him, her breasts came so close to his face he could feel their warmth—

"Landing gear lowered." The shuttle's announcement sounded in the cabin, loud and formal. *Krat.* Drawn roughly back to reality, Carl's feet landed on the floor with a thump.

He checked the instruments again. No problems. Through the plexiglass window, he saw the planet's surface rising rapidly. To one side, about five K from the landing site, was one of those hexagonal structures. The rest of the view was mostly ocean. The RA was to take place at a shoreline.

The sun was coming up, and the RA team would have about five and a half hours before it set. The day promised to be uneventful for Carl, who would wait for the team to take their samples before he had to shuttle them back to the *Galathea*. He wasn't allowed to leave the immediate vicinity of the shuttle in case there was an emergency and they had to make a quick getaway, but that wasn't so bad on this planet. He didn't think he'd ever been anywhere so boring. The shuttle touched down and rolled across the stony beach to a stop.

"Prepare to disembark," Carl said into his mic before pressing the switch to open the airlock. He removed his headset, undid his harness, got up, and pulled on a jacket. They were on a warmer landmass compared to some on the planet, but the temperature remained chilly. By the time he opened the cabin door, the RA team had left, and the passenger cabin was empty but for First Mate Haggardy, who was supervisor this trip. The team was sticking to the master's orders to get a move on and gather their samples and data. Carl went between the rows of seats and out the airlock. He jumped off the ramp, landing roughly on loose pebbles. He staggered.

As he straightened up, he saw that one of the RA team was lingering by the shoreline, her back to the others, who were retrieving their equipment from the hold and setting out to get their samples. Her shoulders were shaking.

Carl went over and stood behind the woman, unsure what to do. He glanced back, but no one else seemed to have noticed her. Gently, he laid a hand on her shoulder. The woman jumped a little and turned to him, hastily wiping her eyes.

"You okay?" Carl asked.

"Yeah," the woman replied. She looked at her feet. "It's just...it isn't how I imagined it would be. Space travel, I mean. I thought it would be exciting, adventurous, you know? But instead it's...kinda..."

"Boring, right? Is this your first mission?"

"Yep. I signed up straight out of college. Everyone else on board seems to have friends already. People they know from previous trips." She looked down again. "I don't seem to fit in anywhere."

Now Carl remembered her. He'd seen her sitting by herself at meals. He'd thought that was what she liked to do, or he would have sat with her. Some people were loners. Was her name Pasha or Sasha? He couldn't remember, and it would be embarrassing to ask. He had a feeling she was with geo-phys.

"You fly the shuttle really well," the woman said. "I hardly felt that landing."

"Huh, the shuttle just about flies...I mean, I trained for five years...to fly starships, and..." He faltered. "Looking forward to a good day...taking...rock samples?"

She laughed. "I don't take rock samples. I operate that." She pointed to a large metal instrument another member of geo-phys was pulling out of the cargo hold. It looked like a device for torturing medium-sized, warm-blooded mammals. Like humans.

"Right," replied Carl, nodding, "I see. And that's a..."

"GPR. Ground Penetrating Radar."

"Hmm..." He rubbed his chin. "Thought I recognized it."

The woman laughed again. "You're funny." She paused a

moment to look at the ocean, then back at Carl. She pulled on an earlobe. "After we get back, I don't suppose..." She paused and looked away. "Do you want to meet up for dinner?"

His eyes widened. "Sure, that'd be great." But where? The ship's refectory was the last place aboard for a potentially romantic dinner. "I tell you what, meet me in the shuttle bay when you've freshened up, and I'll bring something special to eat."

Carl had been hoarding a care package his mother had sent him for the mission. She did it every time he went away. Now would be a good time to break into the tinned and packaged luxury foods.

"Okay," said the woman, smiling. "See you then."

Carl watched as Pasha or Sasha went to the other side of the shuttle to pick up her torture device. She wasn't Harrington, but she seemed really nice and in need of a friend. Harrington was confined to quarters anyway. Personally, he thought the woman's quick temper was sneck, but Loba didn't agree. But Carl wasn't going to pine over her. It wasn't every day a Pasha or Sasha invited you on a date.

THE DAY PASSED SLOWLY for Carl due to the promise of a pleasant evening with the geo-phys scientist. He spent some of the time watching the RA team surveying and sampling the air, plants, water, rocks, sand, and dirt of the planet. He tried not to be too obvious about paying special attention to Pasha or Sasha, but then she and the rest of geo-phys went away over the sand dunes in the direction of the hexagonal structure. After Haggardy fell asleep in the passenger cabin —he hadn't set foot outside the shuttle the entire time—

Carl played the games he'd surreptitiously uploaded to the shuttle's console while he waited for the RA team to return.

As the sun began to set, PashaorSasha came back, walking with the rest of geo-phys as they returned from the alien structure. They'd been gone two or three hours, and Carl wondered what they had all been doing inside the building for so long. The team made their way down the beach dunes, and at the same time other RA members began to straggle back to the shuttle. The sampling session was over. Haggardy sat up and rubbed his eyes, before asking the team members vaguely how the session had gone.

When everyone was aboard, Carl put on his headset and did a final passenger check. He closed the airlock, fastened his harness, and smiled to himself at the promise of an enjoyable dinner ahead.

4

T hree days in her cabin hadn't lessened Jas's anger at Loba for putting his bonus before the crew's safety, but it had evened it out somewhat. If she were to see him, she didn't think she would throw him in a garbage airlock and press Purge right away. She might give him time for some last words first.

She turned on the screen angled above her bunk. A menu of entertainment options appeared: vids, games, music, recorded fly-on-the-wall cam footage, and educational programs. You could watch or play almost anything aboard ship that you could on Earth. The crew of the *Galathea* also had access to mail and videos from home on their private comm systems, options that might have made being cooped up more bearable for Jas, but she had nothing in that vein. No family. No ties to Earth or Mars. At first, she'd thought that made her better off than most others aboard the prospecting ships on their long voyages in deep space. No one to miss and no one to miss her. But over the years, she'd realized that it made it worse. Unlike the rest of the crew, she didn't look forward to the end of a mission.

After a year or longer away from the closest thing she had to home, stepping off the ship with no one to meet her was hard.

She blinked and shook her head. It was no good allowing depressing thoughts to take hold. That was what she hated most about being confined. It gave her time to brood. She needed to *do* something, anything. Her cabin was already spotless, and she'd arranged and rearranged her scant possessions countless times. Looking up at the screen, she could barely focus on it.

Her door chimed. She raised herself on her elbows. Who was risking Loba's wrath by fraternizing with her? Or was it the master himself? She'd told the few crew members she was friendly with to stay away for their own sakes. "Door, open."

Navigator Lee stood waiting. The petite officer was cringing slightly as she looked in.

Jas turned off her screen and swung her legs off her bunk as she sat up. "Come in."

Lee checked from side to side along the corridor before entering the room. She relaxed a little as the door closed behind her.

"Don't want to be seen visiting me, huh?" said Jas. "Wouldn't do much for your reputation, would it?"

Lee looked taken aback. "Maybe I should go." She half-turned.

"Sorry," Jas said. Why did she always push people away? "Don't go. Come and sit down. I'm just stir crazy."

The navigator relented. She pulled out the chair tucked under Jas's desk and sat down. She opened her mouth to speak, but Jas interrupted.

"I'm glad you came. I wanted to thank you for sticking up for me in the mission room. It was brave of you, and I appreciate it. You were the only one who dared side with me against Loba. That took some guts."

The frown on Lee's forehead faded a little. "Thanks, but I wouldn't put it like that. I didn't mind helping you out and all, but I meant what I said. You did save our lives back on 87593g. I've seen you work. You know what you're doing, and if you say 67092d isn't safe I believe you, even if you can't say why. That's what you're paid for, right? To protect us from all those hostile life forms that're out to get us. I mean, what's your incentive for making shit up? What's in it for you? Nothing, right? So if you're saying we need to steer clear, I'm right there beside you. Don't matter what Loba says. There's more important things than money, you know?

"I've read plenty about what can happen to RA teams," Lee continued, "and seen plenty on the news." She gave a shudder. "It ain't safe down there. One of my cousin's friends...or was it someone at his work?...anyway, he knew someone who was just petting a little alien creature for five minutes, and three days later he was dead. Radiation sickness. Wasn't nothing they could do for him. And in another case I heard about, an animal just brushed up against a researcher and ran off. The woman didn't think much of it, but the fur that touched her hand was coated in a poison that penetrated human skin. She lasted a week, and she contaminated a couple of others in her team before they knew about it."

Jas wondered how many more disaster stories Lee had.

"And there was that attack I heard about a while ago," continued Lee. "The ship's security officer didn't even LIV the site the RA team landed at. I heard no one survived. Did you hear about it too? I think they kept it quiet, you know? Didn't want to scare folks? Now, what was that other one...?"

"Yeah, well, like I said," said Jas, standing. "I appreciate the support. Thanks for stopping by." She was beginning to remember why she'd never been more than acquaintances with Navigator Lee.

The navigator smoothed her cropped blonde hair, appearing not to notice Jas's hint. "How have you been? It's been three days now, right? Have you heard anything from the master? Any idea when he might let you out? I'd go crazy sitting in my cabin day after day with no one to talk to. I mean, what on Earth do you do? Do you have comm to the rest of the ship? Can you talk to people?"

Jas sighed and sat down. "No, no contact with the rest of the ship. And you're my first visitor. Loba said something about a mental health assessment, but I haven't heard anything about that either."

"Well, if there is something terrible on that planet, at least it can't get you while you're up here. We're safe here, right?" Lee's eyebrows rose questioningly. When Jas didn't answer, she said, "That's what I think anyway. That's why I never leave the ship."

"You never leave the ship? You've never been planetside? Ever?"

The navigator pinched her lips together and shook her head. "The only planet surface I've ever been on is good ol' Earth. You wouldn't catch me down there. God only knows what might happen."

Jas took a moment to process this statement. "Then...what are you doing here? Why work on a prospecting ship? Why not stay home and get a nice, safe desk job on Earth?"

Lee gave her a questioning look. "Uh, I'm a navigator? My daddy suggested it when I was choosing my degree, and he was right. It's easy for me, and the pay's good. As long as I never leave the ship, I can pretend to myself I only have to step through an airlock to be home."

Jas put her head in her hands. The only supporter she had among all the senior officers was paranoid. What did that say about her? Was she wrong about K. 67092d? Was she crazy too? After her years of service, was she beginning to crack?

"Anyway, I don't like all this talk of hostile aliens," said Lee. "Let's talk about something else. Have you watched *Their Eyes in the Stars* yet? I loved it. Couldn't stop watching it. Had to watch the whole thing through. Took me eleven hours."

Jas's door chime sounded again, and she exhaled with relief, but as she told the door to open, her relief changed to misery. If there was anyone she wanted to see less than Loba, and now Lee, it was the person waiting.

Standing in her cabin entrance, clutching an interface to his chest and smiling a beatific smile, was Sparks. The medical officer was a renowned brown-noser who had clearly decided which section of the crew he favored and which he did not, based on unspoken and unspeakable factors.

He was there for her mental health assessment. Sparks would be itching to have a hand in that.

Lee jumped to her feet, her features confused. She reddened, no doubt embarrassed to be caught in Jas's cabin, but she also seemed pleased to see Sparks. He was definitely glad to see her, if anything could be gleaned from the radiant expression on his face.

"Navigator Lee, what a pleasure to observe you providing comfort to a friend in her hour of need."

The officer's blush faded as she beamed. "I thought C.S.O. Harrington would be lonely in here all by herself."

Sparks's already round eyes widened, and he nodded. "Of course, of course. That was very considerate of you. Do you mind if I join you both?"

"I'm sure you're here for an official reason, Dr. Sparks, so I'll get out of your way," said Lee.

Jas almost regretted it as the navigator left them alone.

"Do you mind if I sit here?" asked the doctor as the door closed behind Lee. He sat in the chair the navigator had vacated. Putting his device face down on the desk, Sparks turned to Jas, leaned forward, put his elbows on his knees, and steepled his fingers. His features assumed an earnest expression. "How have you been?"

"Fine," replied Jas.

Sparks tilted his head and raised his eyebrows. "Have you been sleeping well? Any headaches? Appetite problems?"

"Look, can we cut straight to the mental health check?"

Sparks straightened up. "Hmpf. I'd prefer to do a preliminary general health assessment. It's helpful in order to make an exact diagnosis."

"Is that what this is really about? You've got machines for the general stuff, haven't you? I'm mentally sound, and I'd rather not sit through a load of BF."

Giving her an 'I'm not angry, just disappointed' look, the medical officer picked up his interface and handed it to Jas. "I think we have rather more to talk about than you imagine, Harrington, but if you're refusing to cooperate..." He sighed. "It looks as though your outburst in the mission room was probably a symptom of a serious issue. But let's see the results of the assessment before jumping to conclusions."

He pointed to the first question on the list. "This one is very important."

Jas read the question and scowled. "It's illegal to ask if someone's natural or modded."

"You're right, and for very good reasons of course. But senior medical personnel can make an exception for clinical reasons. A person's genetic status gives essential information about potential mental health issues and other conditions." He spoke in a low tone. "And you can rest easy. Your answer is completely confidential."

The problem was, Jas didn't know if her genes had been modified. Her parents had died in a colony disaster on Mars when she was a baby, and her records were destroyed at the same time. No one in the orphanage had bothered to have her tested, and as she grew up and witnessed the increasing discrimination against naturals, she'd decided against finding out for herself.

She studied the question and looked up at Sparks, who was gazing at her. She didn't believe a word of what he was saying. She thought he was digging about her genetic status so he could slot her into his 'us' and 'them' boxes, but if she didn't pass as mentally fit, she might never get back on duty and find out what was on that planet—before it harmed the crew.

5

***

Retiring to his cabin after his duties were complete was almost Master Akabe Loba's favorite time of day, excepting only what came after. He closed his cabin door, set his corridor-side panel to read *Do Not Disturb* and shrugged off his jacket, dropping it on the floor as he went to his closet. From the top shelf he took a cylindrical container. He popped off the lid and slid out a roll of very old paper, though it might have been another material such as parchment or vellum. Loba was no expert on such things. He sometimes wondered if he'd been duped into paying an exorbitant sum by the vendor, but it didn't matter. If the document was fake, it was convincing to him, and he enjoyed the ancient feel and look of the thing. Most importantly, he had found it to be accurate.

His ritual had been the same as far back as he could remember, though if the truth be told, his memory wasn't as good as it had once been. He should cut down on his habit, he knew, but not today. He would start tomorrow, or next week, when they had cataloged this latest planet, and he could relax a little. Damn that Harrington for causing a delay. He found himself beginning to gasp, and he pushed the memory of the defiant security officer from his mind.

Loba undid and dropped his pants. Stepping out of them, he took two paperweights from the table. One was a fist-sized iridescent crystal he'd picked up from the desert floor of a long-forgotten planet in the days when he'd been working his way up the ranks. The other was a long block of polished ebony: wood of a now-extinct Earth tree. Unfurling the document on the floor, he placed the crystal on one end, then unrolled the rest of the scroll to its full extent before securing the other end with the wooden block.

Every day the same.

Traced in faded ink on the sheet was the figure of a naked man. His arms and legs were outstretched, and his blank eyes were open. Wavy hair surrounded his head like a halo. The figure itself was unimportant to Loba; it was the lines that ran through his body, from his head and spine to his fingertips and toes, that were the focus of his interest. They were meridians: energy paths, where the greatest pain —and pleasure—could be felt.

He ran a fingertip down a line that skirted the groin and followed through to the thigh and leg. It was the meridian he had used for yesterday's dose. To achieve the greatest effect from his drug of choice, Loba had to apply the doses at each point along the meridians according to a strict rota. Yesterday's dose had contacted a point at the left-hand side of his groin. Today, he would administer it fifteen centimeters below, in the thigh. Loba relied on memory alone for the order of the dosing points. If any record of his habit were found, it would be professional suicide. This was why he possessed only a physical document to guide him, a document that could be purged into space in less than a minute. Digital information was much more difficult to erase.

Drug abuse had impacted Loba's functional ability in many areas of his life, but in the matter of remembering the dose position order, his recall was excellent.

He pressed an invisible button on the ebony paperweight. As the block of wood popped open, his breathing quickened. In the lead-lined center of the block was a clear glass vial of carmine liquid. Mythranil. Exquisite purveyor of bliss. Lying next to the vial were a set of fine, hollow needles. Loba could hear himself panting.

Soon, soon.

He removed the vial and a needle and went to the sterilization unit in his bathroom, where he placed the needle in the unit and let it sit for thirty seconds. His hand trembled as he retrieved it.

Only a minute to wait.

He sat on his bunk and removed the stopper from the vial. After inserting the needle in the liquid, he gently sucked at the other end, careful not to draw the mythranil into his mouth. Ingestion destroyed the active ingredients of the drug, and each drop was a week's wages. He slipped the needle from his mouth and quickly placed his thumb over the hole to prevent the liquid from dripping out. Loba took a last look at the image of the spread-eagled man, lay down on his bunk and felt down from the sore spot on his groin to a point roughly fifteen centimeters below.

Just a few seconds now.

Joy suffused Loba as he thrust the needle home, grinning through the pain. His aim was true. He'd hit the meridian line spot on, and ecstasy flowed through him. All cares, worries, and concerns of reality melted away, and he sank into a blissful daze.

LOBA WAS IN NIRVANA. He had achieved a state of perfection. He floated in infinity, where time and space were without end, and where his spirit poured forth and returned replenished, fulfilled, endless, and enduring in the void. Colors with no names whirled through his perception, and indescribable emotions washed over him in blissful waves, cleansing his soul, bathing his mind, washing his ego free of corrupting impurities. For an eternity, it seemed, he existed, each moment filled with limitless joy.

A great bell sounded from behind him. What was this intrusion? Loba turned and tried to gaze into the abyss, but he couldn't find the source of the sound. Again, it rang in his ears, discordant, breaking the serene flow of the universe. He grew confused. Where was the noise coming from? How had it entered the everlasting cosmos?

A third time the bell rang, and Loba cried out as all creation began to disintegrate around him. The terrible noise of the bell was breaking everything apart. He had to find it. He had to stop its chiming before it was too late. He had to destroy it.

Loba flailed in his bunk so hard he fell out and hit the floor with a thump. The shock and pain of his fall brought him somewhat back to reality, and he realized the sound he'd been hearing, which had intruded into his drug-induced state of euphoria, was his door chime. But it was too soon. Someone had disturbed him before the effects of mythranil had worn off.

As if at the flick of a switch, Loba's mood altered from befuddlement to black rage. He took a moment to figure out where each of his limbs were before rising to a crouch and staggering to his feet. Hands trembling and chest heaving, he snatched the meridian map from the floor and put it in his closet before shutting the door. He put the vial of mythranil and needle into the ebony box and snapped it closed.

He staggered to his cabin door just as the chime sounded for the fourth time. Whoever it was, the idiot still hadn't realized the grave mistake he was making. Loba turned on his video link to the corridor. A woman. A member of an RA team. He couldn't remember her name. "Door, open.

"What the hell do you think you're doing?" he bellowed. "Are you blind or stupid? How dare you disturb me..." Loba tailed off. The woman was speaking at the same time as him, apparently unaffected by his anger.

She repeated herself when he paused. "Master Loba, we found something on the planet surface you need to see urgently."

"What? Now? What the hell's so important...?"

"I can't explain. You must come with me to the planet. You must come with me immediately."

"The hell I'm going to. I'm not going anywhere. Explain yourself. What is this about? What did you find there? Pah, I don't care what it is. File a report like you're supposed to and stop bothering me..." The world spun. He grabbed the door frame.

"It's very important," the woman said. "Very valuable. You must come with me and see for yourself. There's no other way."

What was wrong with her? Why wouldn't she obey him? He was master. Loba clutched his head. Was this even real? Or was he still in a mythranil dream? His initial fury began to melt into bewilderment and confusion. Maybe he should go with the woman. If this was all part of his vision, he might return to bliss by doing what she said.

He peered at her. Why hadn't she reacted to his fury? He felt chilly, and with sudden horror, he realized he was standing there in his underwear. The woman hadn't reacted to that either.

Calm descended on Loba. None of it was real. He was still under the influence of mythranil. But it was strange. He'd never run like this before. Maybe he'd gotten the dosage or position wrong. He would just have to go with the flow, see the vision through, and then perhaps he would return to paradise for some time before he woke up.

"Okay, I'll come with you."

The woman seemed satisfied.

6

———

Carl was in the middle of destroying the evil mastermind behind the invasion of Planet Zytron when someone rang his door chime.

"Better hide, mate," he said to a pale brown, furry creature that was clinging to an air vent with his feet and wing hooks. The animal looked like something between a bat and a sugar glider, and it had been Carl's friend since childhood. Ship's pets were strictly prohibited on any Polestar vessel, but Carl had always thought little Flux would never cause any harm, so it was no big deal if he smuggled him aboard.

"Righto," the creature replied, and flew across the room to an open cupboard. He went inside and a wing hook appeared, gripped the door edge, and pulled it nearly closed.

Carl had gone to bed disappointed and hungry after PashaorSasha had failed to show for their date at the shuttle bay. Video games were poor compensation for female company, but he'd concluded that if something seemed too good to be true, it probably was, though he couldn't understand why the woman would go to the trouble of inviting him on a date only to stand him up. Some people were weird.

He frowned and checked the time. Who could it be at this hour? Had PashaorSasha had second thoughts? Or maybe she'd been delayed and come over to apologize for the no show? A small flame of hope flickered. He leapt up and put on his shirt.

He stepped into his pants and, pulling them up, he hopped to the door. As he opened it, his heart sped up. It *was* the geo-phys scientist. "Hi, great to see you. What happened...?" His face fell. Master Loba was a short distance away in the corridor. "Sir," he said, buttoning up his shirt, but the man didn't reply. He looked out of it.

"You have to take us planetside," said PashaorSasha

"What?" Carl's fingers hesitated. "You want me to fly you down there right now?"

"Yes. Immediately. The master must go to the planet, to the site we were at today. There's something I have to show him."

"But that's, that's..." Carl scratched his scalp. Was it even daylight at that site right now? He didn't know off the top of his head. He looked at the master again. Loba was leaning against the corridor wall, his white curls mussed up, and his eyes didn't seem to be focusing too well. Carl had heard the rumors.

He pushed his shirt into his pants slowly, buying time to think. It was all completely against protocol. *Teams* went down to the planet, not just two people, and it had to be for a legitimate reason. No tourist trips. Polestar didn't fund deep space vacations. If geo-phys had found something, there was a process to follow. But this was Loba's order, and the man was known for his vindictiveness. If Carl disobeyed without good reason, there would be serious consequences.

Stepping into the corridor, he closed his door before going over to Loba. "Sir, is this right? You want me to take you planetside?"

The master seemed to take a moment to realize that the pilot was there. He pushed himself off the wall and wavered as he stood upright. "Take us...me and her..." He pointed at PashaorSasha. "Now. Special assignment."

Carl's frown melted away as everything became clear to him. PashaorSasha had stood him up because she'd had a better offer. The master of a starship, no less. And now she wanted him to take her and her new boyfriend on a drugged-out trip to an alien planet. *Great.*

"Right. I get it. Fine, just fine." What could he do but agree? He didn't want to kiss his career goodbye. If he refused, it would mean no flying starships through deep space. No sneck uniform. No female crew members to impress.

"Come on then," he called over his shoulder as he strode away toward the shuttle deck. He knew he shouldn't talk to the master like that, but the fool was too off his face to notice, probably.

PashaorSasha and the master didn't act like a couple who were hot for each other, Carl noticed as the two came with him and finally sat down in the shuttle's passenger cabin, but maybe that was their kink. Maybe they were role-playing. His heart sank lower at the thought that *he* could have been the one pretending to be on 'official business' with PashaorSasha.

Taking his pilot seat, he contacted the bridge. His request for clearance to fly was met with predictable confusion. Of course, the lust-sick master hadn't informed them of his plans. Carl switched his mic to broadcast in the passenger cabin. "Sir, bridge requires your personal order. You'll need to step into my cabin."

A few moments later, after fumbling with the door, Loba appeared, looking a little more alert and focused. Taking the spare headset Carl handed him, he spoke into the mic. "This is Master Loba. I...er...I authorize this trip, for...er...scientific reasons." He blinked and looked at Carl as if he were recognizing him for the first time.

After a small delay, the 'clear' signal flashed on Carl's controls as he heard the spoken confirmation. Loba's verbal order must have passed the security check. Myth clearly didn't impact the voice much.

The master's hand was resting on the back of Carl's flight seat. The man hesitated, as if he were about to speak, but he retreated to the passenger cabin.

With more force than necessary, Carl flipped the take-off switches and input the previous day's coordinates into the flight plan. Would it be night or day at the site by the time they touched down? He didn't have any idea. Would it matter for what PashaorSasha and the master had planned?

Carl thrust the clips of his harness home.

LOBA'S HEAD WAS CLEARING. Something was very, very wrong. The mythranil was wearing off. His run was coming to an end, and he hadn't returned to bliss by following the woman. Her interruption of his vision, his requesting the copilot fly them to the surface, and their boarding the shuttle—none of it had been the effects of the drug. It had all been real.

The shuttle had landed. Loba unfastened his belt and got up unsteadily before following the geo-phys scientist to the open air lock. An icy breeze hit him as he stood on the shuttle's ramp in the pre-dawn light. He shivered. He wasn't dressed for such weather. He was wearing only the uniform that he wore aboard ship. What the hell was he doing here? He hadn't set foot on an alien planet in years.

The woman was already walking away into the gloom. She was determined to show him something, but what? What could possibly be so important, so valuable, to drag your master from his bed and all the way to the mission planet?

His first impulse was to order the scientist back, return to the warmth of the shuttle's passenger cabin, and direct the copilot to fly them back to the ship, but he considered that might not be the best path of action. The trip was already unorthodox, outside of company regulations. He would face additional scrutiny from his officers if he aborted the expedition as soon as he arrived. They would be too cautious to say anything outright, but his behavior would be rich fodder for anyone who wanted to accuse him of incompetency.

Secondly, his curiosity was piqued. Had the woman found something truly remarkable; something that really did deserve his scrutiny, and his scrutiny alone? Perhaps it was a find that would make him so rich he could buy enough mythranil to last a lifetime.

He started after the scientist. She was heading over the dunes in the direction of one of those structures Harrington had been investigating. Those places she had been getting her panties in a twist over. *Misborn.* Her excessive caution had been a thorn in his side this whole mission. He wouldn't hire her again, and he'd write an unfavorable reference if anyone asked. He hoped she'd failed the mental health assessment he'd ordered the doctor to give her. The report was due in the morning. If she passed, maybe he could persuade Sparks to tweak the results. The man was usually quick to pick up on hints.

Loba caught up with the geo-phys woman. She didn't speak as he fell into step beside her, seemingly intent on reaching the structure as quickly as possible.

"What is it you're going to show me?" he asked. "Is it a new mineral? Or something very rare? What's important enough to bring me here?"

When she didn't answer, Loba's temper rose. As always, coming down from mythranil left him fragile and moody. "I command you to tell me immediately." He grabbed the woman's shoulder and spun her round. She slipped on the sand and fell to her knees. Her expression unchanging, she rose to her feet.

"You have to come with me," she said, and went on. It was all she would say, no matter how much Loba quizzed her.

They reached the structure. The pre-dawn glow faintly gilded the edges of the hexagonal blocks but didn't penetrate the dark interior.

The woman went inside, turning on a flashlight she had brought with her. Exasperated beyond words, Loba followed, brushing the wall with his fingertips as he entered. The material was glassy, smooth, and cold. The master shivered and hoped it was warmer inside.

Within the room they'd entered was another opening. The woman immediately passed through it, and Loba followed. The next room was identical to the last, except the floor sloped downward. The woman quickly took the nearest doorway again, and again, and again. Loba could barely keep up as she led him deeper and deeper within the structure. Soon, he was completely lost. Sometimes only the beams from her flashlight told him where the woman had gone. He called out to her as they went, telling her to slow down, asking where they were going, how much farther they had to go, what they were going to see, but she never answered. He ordered her to stop, on pain of dismissal, but it was as if she didn't hear him for all the notice she took.

Did the scientist know where she was going? The structure seemed larger than it had looked on the outside. But maybe they were now underground. Loba was very tired. Mythranil sped up the metabolism and sapped the user's energy levels, and he hadn't eaten his usual post-run high calorie breakfast. The cold seemed to bite his very bones. He begged the woman to stop so that he could rest. He staggered on through another few rooms. Then, before he knew it, she was gone. He was in complete darkness. He shouted for the woman. There was no answer. He was deep within the structure. He was exhausted, hypothermic, thirsty, and hungry, and he didn't know the way out.

Loba collapsed onto his hands and knees. For a moment, the ache of his muscles distracted him from a strange tingling in his palms, but the sensation grew stronger and more unpleasant. He gasped in pain and tried to lift his hands from the floor, but he couldn't move them. It was as if they were stuck with a strong adhesive. He pulled harder. It felt like he was pulling off his skin. He cried out in agony. His hands had somehow become melded with the floor. Loba whimpered and wept. He shouted for the woman to return to help him, for anyone to help him. His hands were on fire.

Even the edges of his sleeves were stuck to the floor. They were sinking in. His hands were sinking in, too. The floor was absorbing his hands.

"Nooooo," screamed Loba. "Nooooo, help me, please. I'll do anything. I'll give you everything I have. Pleeeeeease."

As his wrists and arms began to disappear, he fought and flailed, flinging his body backward and forward in an effort to free himself. He would have broken his bones, torn his own skin off, to free himself, but he could not. His writhings brought his cheek in contact with the alien surface. Immediately, his face was stuck. It also began to sink in. Jaw, then cheek disappeared. The edge of his lips reached the floor. Loba shrieked incoherently until his mouth and nose were absorbed. After that, only the muffled noise made by his slowly disappearing vocal chords could be heard.

7

Lying on her back in her bunk, her arm over her face, Jas groaned quietly to herself. The mental health assessment hadn't gone well. In fact, it'd gone very badly. She could have sworn that Sparks had been deliberately, subtly antagonizing, but also, just maybe, she'd let her emotions get the better of her.

Her memory of the encounter was painfully clear.

He didn't believe her. Despite all her explanations about how the records of her conception were lost, how she'd spent her first few years in a government institution on Mars, how she'd never wanted to have herself tested, she could tell from his expression that he thought she was a natural, and she was lying to cover up the fact.

He gave her a patronizing look, rested a hand on her knee, and said, "You don't need to say any more. I understand your caution, but it isn't as if you can help it, is it? We can't choose our parents, after all, nor their economic situation. Don't worry. As I said, the answers you give are completely confidential." He leaned closer. "I won't tell a soul."

The force with which Jas knocked his hand away was a little too strong, because Sparks fell forward and toppled to the floor. As he got to his feet, his practiced mask of serene benevolence broke for a moment. He scowled before regaining his composure. He straightened his tunic and resumed his seat. Raising a hand, he said, "I understand this is a difficult subject for you. No need to apologize."

Jas hadn't been about to apologize. "I've told you as much as I know about my genetic status, okay? I'll answer the rest of the questions." She pressed the fingerprint scanner on the interface screen. Her name flashed up as the device registered her identity. She skimmed the questions. Did she ever wish to harm herself or others? She threw a hooded glance at Sparks as she pressed no. Did she ever feel restless, agitated, tense, or frantic? Only when confined to her cabin for three days. No.

It was standard, obvious stuff. Anyone with half a brain could fake their answers to make it appear they were functioning normally. Jas answered as she thought someone who wasn't mentally ill would answer, with one or two slightly questionable responses just in case the test was set up to identify fakers. Most of her answers were true anyway.

She handed the interface back to Sparks. "Don't you have a brain scan for this kind of thing these days?"

"Not yet, though I believe they're working on it. But we do have a physical assessment. The physician interprets the results."

"What?" Jas scooted back a little on her bunk. Sparks was going to examine her? And it was up to him to say if she passed? It was game over. The man couldn't tell the difference between the thermatic plague of K.76309c and the common cold, and even if he were competent, there was no way he would clear her as mentally fit now that he thought she was a natural.

"Can I refuse?"

Sparks smiled. "Who in their right mind would refuse?"

Jas grimaced and turned onto her side as she recalled

what happened next. Sparks had shone a small flashlight in her eyes and tracked her eye movement. He'd tested her reflexes and made her go through a set of physical exercises. She'd grown gradually angrier. What he was asking her to do was ridiculous. She'd suspected he was making it all up. Playing with her. Finally, she'd lost her temper.

"I'm not taking any more of this. Get out."

The doctor was in the middle of keying his findings into his interface. He looked up. "What?"

"You aren't going to pass me no matter what I do, are you? Get out of my cabin."

Sparks looked amused. "I appear to have upset you." He brought his hands together as if in prayer. "I'm so sorry." A slight smirk appeared on his lips.

The smirk had been the final straw. She'd grabbed him, opened her door and pushed him into the corridor.

Jas shook her head. She was an idiot. If she'd just played ball, if she'd just lied and said she was modded, she might have been back on duty the next day. Finding out what it was on that planet should have been her focus. She shouldn't have let that obsequious, two-faced bigot get to her.

She sighed and her arm fell to her side. Opening her eyes, she gazed, unseeing, at the low ceiling. How was she going to protect the crew? She had to do something, but what? She had to get out of her cabin, for a start. She couldn't do anything trapped in there.

She turned on her bunk screen to check the time. It was the quiet shift. Most of the crew would be asleep. She might be able to get around the ship without being seen if she were careful. But where to go? The answer was obvious. The danger was on the planet. If she could get down there and continue her investigations, she might find something concrete she could show the master; if she displayed the evidence in front of the other officers—something he couldn't ignore—he would be forced to act.

There was only one way to get planetside. She removed her comm button, which contained a tracer, and placed it on her bunk.

A SHORT DETOUR TO collect one of the defense units was worth the additional risk of being seen, Jas decided. If she encountered something dangerous, she would need all the help she could get.

No one crossed her path in the ship's corridors on her way to the unit storage room. The defense units were all exactly as she'd left them, facing each other in two rows on either side of the room in the dark, as they always were when not in use. She'd often wondered if they ever spoke to each other while they were alone.

"AX10, come with me."

One of the figures turned and moved toward her.

"Close the door," she said over her shoulder as she left. The unit's footfalls were heavy as it followed her to the shuttle bay.

She was in luck. The door to the hold on the shuttle had been left open. She climbed into the dark, bare, metallic interior and directed AX10 to do the same. Stowing away in the passenger or pilot areas was out of the question. There was nowhere large enough for her to hide, and definitely nowhere the defense unit would fit. But tucked in a corner of the equipment hold they wouldn't be easily seen. The RA teams wouldn't check the interior before throwing in their equipment.

She'd brought along her combat suit. As soon as she heard the crew arrive for the next assessment trip in the morning, she would suit up. Though the hold offered some protection from the extremes of space, she stood a good chance of dying if she wasn't wearing a suit, and though the planet's atmosphere had been cleared fit to breathe, she might need the suit's protection.

She lay down and rested her head on the unit's thigh while she waited. Its large, firm muscles didn't make much of a pillow, but it was better than nothing. In a way, being uncomfortable was a benefit. She couldn't risk falling asleep.

"Hey, AX10."

"Yes, C.S.O. Harrington?"

"Do you units talk to each other when you're alone?"

"We do not."

"Why not?" Long experience of working with defense units had taught Jas she was on shaky ground asking one of them a 'why' question, but she needed to stay awake.

"We have nothing to say, C.S.O. Harrington."

Jas was about to ask another question, but she snapped her mouth closed. Footsteps. Someone was entering the shuttle bay. More than one person. It sounded like two or three. She sat up. What was going on? It was much too early for an assessment trip. The starship was on down-time, geostationary above the side of the planet currently facing away from the sun so the scanners could take night-state readings.

Whoever was in the shuttle bay, they weren't talking. The footsteps were headed toward the shuttle. Surely they weren't going to board and fly out?

She couldn't take any chances. Jas grabbed her suit and hastily began to put it on. She thrust her legs and arms into the holes and sealed the front. She froze. Someone was walking toward the hold. She couldn't see the door from her position, but she heard it swing down and clunk closed. She was in pitch darkness before her helmet light blinked on. The floor began to vibrate as the engines started up. The shuttle lifted, and she was tossed onto her side. She clipped her helmet in place and pulled down the visor just in time as they entered space.

8

———

Deep within the alien structure, a bulge appeared in the wall of a chamber. The bulge swelled and rippled. It took shape. The shape of a human head. Colored the matte gray of the surrounding wall, the head turned from side to side, and its as-yet unseeing eyes opened, also a uniform gray. The mouth gaped in a silent scream. A neck, shoulders, and a torso emerged. Arms broke free. Below the torso a gray knee appeared, followed by a thigh and foot. A leg took a step out of the wall, the foot gripping the floor for traction, and dragged the rest of the body out after it.

The figure stood, unsteady, as color bled across its surface and the facial features refined. Hair grew from the head, swirling into white curls. Cloth rose from the skin and separated from it, forming clothes. The creature breathed in for the first time, and needles of fiery pain spread from its opening lungs.

Ah, an atmosphere-breathing organism with a nervous system. Exquisite agony. To breathe, to feel again, after eons of confinement.

Nerves spasmed into life, sending signals from the being's periphery, information about ambient temperature and the movement of air. The sensations were unpleasant. The environment was too cold for this organism. The material that covered the creature also stimulated its nerve endings, though the sensation was more satisfying. The cloth captured the animal's heat and protected it from the cold.

The heart beat once, twice, and settled into a steady rhythm. Newly formed blood moved sluggishly then faster through opening veins and arteries. The visual organs, the eyes, remained unstimulated. The creature speculated that light must be required for them to operate. Outside, they should work more effectively.

Two limbs...legs...adjoined the lower half of the body, and two more sprang from the upper half. Arms. The being moved its legs and toppled to the ground. More pain. It lifted itself up and balanced again. The legs appeared to be the only method of locomotion. It tried again and fell once more.

A short time later, the creature took a few staggering steps. Once it had succeeded in this task, its learning was exponential. Within a few minutes, it began to walk confidently. After encountering a wall and experiencing pain, it used its arms to supplement the poor quality of information coming from its visual organs. The arms had many nerves at their far ends, in the hands and fingers, and the creature navigated its way in the darkness, using them to locate obstructions.

The sensation of being separate was strange, and it took some time for the creature to reconcile the information it received from its nerves with its previous experience of being at one with the structure and the void beyond it, and the others of its kind. But in time it perceived the building as a discrete entity, and that it was located inside. At this realization, it ceased wandering randomly and began to work its way to the surface.

As the being went, it grew accustomed to its new mind, and millions of pieces of information began to manifest, drawn from the alien life form the structure had absorbed. Memories, knowledge, language. Certain vocalizations were very important. The creature opened its mouth, moved its lips and tongue. Brand-new vocal cords, moist and fresh, vibrated.

"Ah-kah-be-lo-ba."

A name. A sound signifying a thing. It was the name of the absorbed creature. But the sound was not quite right. "Akabe." Pause. "Loba." That was correct.

Visual signals from the eyes were strengthening. The light around the creature was growing brighter. It was nearing the exterior. In its mind, neurons fired, channels of information flew open, and new torrents of information poured forth. The animal called its species *human*. The species was dimorphous. The absorbed creature had been of the type called male, or man. It had been the most important man on a vessel that traveled between the stars. An autonomous reaction from the nervous system fired, and pleasure flooded the creature.

The light intensity grew bright as the creature neared the structure's exit. Its eyes didn't adjust quickly enough, and pain registered. It closed its eyelids halfway. Waiting at the exit was one of the others from which it had separated, and this one had also transformed into a human. It was a female of the species, and it had brought Master Akabe Loba to the structure to be replicated.

As the creature joined the female, the pair did not speak.

They had no need, for their minds were one. Only their newly adopted physical forms were separate—a temporary, necessary inconvenience. First, they must bring more humans from the orbiting starship to the structures for absorption. If most of the humans were not consumed and copied, their entity would face dangerous hostilities. They also needed many more copies of humans and other alien species on the physical plain to achieve their final goal.

Outside, the movement of the cold air was brisk and uncomfortable. The creature began to shiver. The other led the way to the vessel that would take them to the starship. The shuttlecraft was small, but it looked well made. An attractive item of technology and likely to be only one of many more the humans had created. A vista of replication, domination, acquisition, and, ultimately, complete control of this physical expanse opened in the creatures' shared mind.

It was time for generation to begin.

9

Jas waited, squatting on her heels. When the shuttle had landed, and she'd heard the ramp descend and two sets of footsteps walk down it, then silence. She racked her brains as to what was going on, but none of it made any sense. Two people weren't enough for an RA team, and the teams weren't due out until morning anyway. An RA team also wouldn't go on a trip without equipment. She wondered if Lingiari had taken the shuttle on a whim and flown down with a friend. But he would never have gotten clearance from the bridge, and even Lingiari wasn't stupid enough to fly without clearance. He'd be sacked and blacklisted in the industry forever.

Who had the authority to order an unscheduled visit to the planet? Only Loba. But why on Earth would he do it? His was the archetypal hands-off, don't-bother-me approach.

The circle of light from Jas's headlamp wobbled on the bare, metallic equipment hold floor as her head shook slightly in perplexity. AX10 remained motionless behind her. With no room to stand up, she crawled toward the door.

She swept her headlamp's rays across the door's seams. As she expected, there was no way to open it from the inside.

She sat back. She'd come here for a reason. Could she continue as planned, despite the odd circumstances?

"AX10, can you connect to the shuttle's computer system?"

"Affirmative, C.S.O. Harrington."

"Tell it to open the hold. You can do that, right?" She didn't know if the two who had descended the ramp were still around. They'd had enough time to leave the area. If they were still near the shuttle, they might interpret the hold door opening to be a glitch. It was a chance she was prepared to take.

"I can," said the unit. "Do you want me to do that?"

"Ye—wait." Jas had worked with defense units long enough to get to know their ways. They were intelligent, but they lacked empathy and theory of mind. It might be necessary for them to kill intelligent, sentient species, and the ability to imagine how another creature was feeling and thinking would make them inefficient. But the units' mental foibles also meant they struggled to imagine how information available to them might be useful to someone else. Jas had learned that, as a result, they had a kind of fail-safe. They would check an order if they knew something that they suspected might jeopardize the maneuver. "What might I need to know, AX10?"

"We are not traveling in the passenger cabin; therefore, I believe we are hiding. I do not know if the pilot should be aware of our location. If I tell the shuttle's computer to open the door, it will communicate the action to him."

"You mean it'll announce, *AX10 is opening the hold door?*"

"Affirmative, C.S.O. Harrington."

Krat. Assuming it was Lingiari who'd flown the shuttle—

she didn't think the main pilot, Grantwise, would agree to such an unorthodox trip—he might still be aboard. She didn't want to get Lingiari in trouble, but on the other hand, if she couldn't get out and look around, the safety of the entire crew might be at stake. Also, once Lingiari knew he had a defense unit on board, he might guess she was accompanying it and not come into the hold with weapons blazing.

"Okay, AX10, go for it. Tell the shuttle to open the hold door."

A moment later, with a clunk and a judder, the door swung up. Gray light filled the hold. An ocean moved outside, waves sweeping the shore. Jas opened her visor to make it easier for Lingiari to recognize her. A tangy odor accompanied the chill breeze from the water. Pale stars winked in the pre-dawn light.

Slow, heavy footsteps came down the ramp. He was taking his time. Jas rolled her eyes. If Lingiari's hold were filled with murderous aliens, they would have killed him three minutes ago. She would have to upgrade the crew's combat training. A man's lanky figure came into view, silhouetted against the sky, his hand gripping a small weapon.

"Lingiari," Jas whispered, just loud enough to be heard above the ocean, "it's me."

"Harrington?" The pilot's broad, honest features became visible and brightened as he stepped closer. "What the hell?"

She climbed out and jumped down from the hold. "Shhh...is anyone else around?"

"No. Loba and the geo-phys woman left ten minutes ago."

"So it is Loba. And he's with Margret?"

"No, Pasha, or Sasha. I can't remember her name."

"There's only one woman with geo-phys, and her name's Margret Stratton."

"Oh, in that case, yeah, Margret. They're tagging up over there somewhere." He waved toward the dunes, a disappointed look on his face.

"Loba and Margret? BF."

"Yeah, they are. Why else would Loba make me fly them down?"

"Lingiari, were you born on Balgamon? Loba probably hasn't raised the flag in years. That's the first thing to go when you're running the blood."

The pilot's eyes widened. "Glad I never tried it." He looked at her intently. "No myth's affected my ability. Everything's working fine down there."

Jas frowned. Why was he telling her that? He had a weird look on his face.

Lingiari continued, "So Loba let you out your cabin?"

"Not exactly. I snuck out and stowed away so I could check out the planet some more. There's something not right here. I have to find out what it is."

Lingiari rubbed his head. "You mean you're still confined to quarters?"

"Yeah. You won't say anything, will you?"

The pilot hesitated, then said, "No, 'course not. I won't dob on you. I've always liked you, Harrington."

There was that weird look again.

"Err...thanks, Lingiari. You said they went over there?"

"Yeah. They didn't say when they'd be back, but I hope it's soon. I need to get back to the ship and pick up the RA team. It'll be daylight in a couple of hours."

"I'm going to see what I can find. Don't take off without me, okay? Can you scan the hold for life forms?" The copilot nodded. "Good. Check we're on board before you take off. I'll try to get back before Loba and Margret."

Telling AX10 to follow, Jas set off at a lope toward the dunes. Following the direction Lingiari had indicated, Jas scrambled upward, slipping on the stones and sand. As her head crowned the rise she was greeted by the sight she'd feared. About a kilometer away was one of the hexagonal structures. It was no surprise. They were dotted across all the planet's landmasses. The ship's scanners had even detected a few on the ocean floor. She was sure it was in the structures that the danger lay, whatever it was.

Loba and Margret were nowhere to be seen, which meant they must have gone inside. She couldn't follow them into the building. If Loba saw her, it would all be over.

She debated returning to the shuttle and waiting for Loba and Margret to return, but there was no rush. She would have plenty of time to get back as soon as she spotted them. She decided to observe the landscape while she was there. After pulling down her visor, she activated its zoom and checked her surroundings in detail.

Lingiari was walking up and down the shoreline, his hands in his pockets, kicking the sand. Beyond him, a group of small creatures briefly lifted out of the ocean waves. Nearby, slime molds inched along among the rough dune plants. AX10 was squatting, still and silent, awaiting his next order.

After more than an hour's observation, Jas concluded there seemed nothing threatening outside the artificial structure. Her bored gaze returned to it. Why had Margret taken Loba there? Had she discovered the threat and wanted to show him personally?

The approaching sun gilded the horizon. Movement at an opening in the building made her freeze. The swiftly rising sun's beams illuminated two figures emerging. Loba and Margret. They'd done whatever they'd come to do and were returning to the shuttle.

Jas watched them approach. Lingiari's theory that the two were tagging up was ridiculous. And they certainly didn't behave like a couple in love, or lust. They were walking a short distance apart and not even looking at each other. They also didn't appear to be talking.

Something was weird about their gait. It was familiar, but it didn't look right. For a moment, Jas couldn't figure out what it was, then it came to her. They were walking like defense units. Their steps were almost mechanical, and they were facing consistently forward with no interest in what was around them. She watched them as they covered nearly the whole distance to the dunes, but their behavior didn't change.

Frowning, Jas took one last look before slipping back to the shuttle.

10

Navigator Sayen Lee straightened her pillow and smoothed the covers on her bunk until they were free of folds and creases. She felt a little queasy. Was she coming down with a stomach virus? Or was it food poisoning? She'd had the Asiatic option for breakfast: congee, pickled vegetables, steamed bun and soy milk. The pickled cabbage had tasted a little strange. She wouldn't be surprised if the chief steward cut corners when it came to food hygiene, under pressure from the master to save money.

Sitting down at her desk, Sayen said, "Open interface," and the entire desk surface became a screen filled with numbers and mathematical characters. Sayen was about halfway through the calculations for the next starjump on the *Galathea's* schedule. She didn't actually need to do the calculation herself. The ship's computer would do it, but she figured it out herself every time anyway, for relaxation. Her result always matched the computer's.

Her math professor at college had seen her doing a starjump calculation one day, and after looking over her shoulder for a few minutes had asked her what it was. When Sayen explained, the woman laughed and told her not to be ridiculous; that the computation was beyond the ability of a single human being and it would take years to work it out.

Sayen had shrugged and said she'd figured out a few short cuts. The professor had smiled condescendingly and replied, "Yes, of course you have," before walking away, shaking her head and laughing.

It hadn't mattered to Sayen then that her professor didn't believe her, and it didn't matter now. On the rare occasions she'd been the center of attention, she'd felt uncomfortable. She had no incentive in broadcasting her abilities; she was content to use them as necessary to secure a high-paying job, but no more.

Sayen studied the calculation and worked on it for some time before she realized that she was due on the bridge soon. Closing the screen, she stood and faced a wall of her cabin. "Mirror." The wall became reflective and displayed an image of a petite woman with short, blonde, razor-cut hair, wearing an immaculate Polestar uniform. She checked her clothes for spots and lint, turning and looking over her shoulder to see the reflection of her back.

Sayen's stomach churned a little, and she put a hand to it. She would have to pay Dr. Sparks a short visit before her shift started. She still had time if she hurried. She had one last thing to do before leaving her cabin, however: the final stage of her morning routine.

She went into her shower room to wash her hands, but as she passed through the door, she remembered she'd run out of hand sanitizer. Her face fell. What was she going to do? She always washed her hands before going to work. Always. But the last time she'd asked the chief steward for an extra bottle of sanitizer he'd told her that was the last one she was allowed.

There was nothing else she could do, she would just have to skip visiting the doctor and go see the chief steward instead. He had to give her some more sanitizer. He had to.

She stepped out of her cabin in a hurry and walked straight into Lingiari, the copilot. The two collided. Lingiari was barely affected by the impact, but Sayen bounced off the rangy man and nearly fell down. At the same time, Lingiari gave a great sneeze, showering Sayen in a spittle spray.

"Oughh," she exclaimed, wrinkling her nose. "That's disgusting." She wiped her face with her hands and looked down at her uniform.

"Sorry," said the copilot. "I wasn't expecting you to pop out like that."

Sayen backed away, wiping her hair and each hand in turn. "Do you have a cold? Don't tell me you have a cold."

"I don't think so, I just...got a bit..." He gestured behind him in the direction of the shuttle bay. He appeared to be about to say something, then changed his mind. "I don't think I've got a cold."

"Oughh." Sayen gave a slight shudder and went around Lingiari, giving him a very wide berth.

The chief steward's office was on the other side of the ship. She would have to hurry if she wasn't going to be late for her shift. She quickly turned a corner, but stopped. Harrington was coming toward her. C.S.O. Harrington, who was supposed to be confined to her cabin. The security officer was racing down the corridor.

"What are you—" asked Sayen.

"Shhh," hissed Harrington as she passed by, "don't tell

anyone. Please don't, and I promise if you ever need protecting from aliens, I'll be right there."

"Oh, I...okay," she said to the security officer's retreating figure.

Today was turning out to be odd. But she didn't have time to figure out what was going on. She had to get to the chief steward. Fifteen minutes later, panting, she pressed his door chime.

"Who is it?" came the man's voice over the intercom.

"Sayen Lee."

There was a sigh of exasperation. "What is it this time? Disinfectant? Polish? Sanitizer?"

"That's it. I need some more sanitizer. I know you—"

"No. I've already told you. No more. Use the UV box like everyone else. Sanitizer is redundant and outdated. That's why we—"

"But I really need it. If no one else—"

"No."

"But—"

"No."

The light on the intercom went out. The chief steward had turned it off.

Panic rose in Sayen's throat. She had to wash her hands. A disaster would happen if she didn't. What kind of disaster, she didn't know, but it would be something really bad.

Sayen went back the way she'd come. Where could she get some hand sanitizer? The communal restrooms didn't have any. They only had UV boxes. And what good were they? On one level she knew they were the most efficient way of killing germs, but she didn't feel right using them; she didn't feel hygienic. She needed that reassurance of spreading sanitizer all over her hands and the tingle of it evaporating.

The corridors were filling with crew members on their way to their workstations. Maybe one of them could help? There had to be someone else on board who still liked to use hand sanitizer. She stopped and scanned the faces as they passed. At last, she saw someone who might be able to help—Sayen had introduced herself only the day before as the woman had seemed lonely—though now she didn't seem to have noticed her.

"Hi. It's Margret, right?" asked Sayen as the geo-phys scientist had almost passed by. When she didn't stop, Sayen grabbed her arm. Margret turned slowly, as if she were in a trance or deep in thought.

"Margret, I'm Sayen, remember?" she said when the woman still didn't seem to recognize her. "I was wondering if you have any hand sanitizer?"

"Hand sanitizer," echoed Margret.

"Yes, do you have any?"

"No, I don't have hand sanitizer."

Sayen peered into Margret's face. Her expression was blank. "Are you feeling okay?"

Margret didn't reply, but began to walk away. Sayen followed her. "Are you sure you don't have any? Could you check? Hey, I think your cabin's this way," she said as Margret took a wrong turn into the storage section. Something was definitely wrong with her. She would have to tell Dr. Sparks. After grabbing the woman's hand, she led her the right way.

They arrived at Margret's cabin. As soon as they were through the door, Sayen went into the shower room. Her heart leapt. There it was, on the side of the basin: a nearly full bottle.

11

———

Jas's cabin walls seemed to close around her after she returned from stowing away on the shuttle. The few hours' freedom had been a welcome break from confinement, despite the deeply worrying revelation that the master of the *Galathea* was now compromised.

Both Loba and Margret had been acting as if they were in a kind of trance. There was no doubt in Jas's mind that something was within the artificial structures on K. 67092d, something neither she nor the defense units had spotted in all the LIVs they'd conducted. What they'd missed was still a mystery, but as far as she was concerned, her initial suspicions had been vindicated. The problem was, she was the only person aboard who understood that at least two crew members had been infected by an alien organism, and that the rest of them were in danger. Though Lingiari had acknowledged something wasn't right, he hadn't been convinced the threat was serious enough to raise an alarm.

How could she convince anyone to listen to her? Her reputation was at an all-time low. None of the officers would believe what she had to say. And if she told anyone she'd been planetside, she'd be put in the brig and dismissed, or even prosecuted and fined when they returned to Earth, assuming they made it that far. Her only hope was Lingiari. She'd asked him to come to her cabin when his shift was over. She was sure he'd show. He'd seemed enthusiastic about the idea. She had to talk him into trying to alert the others that something was wrong with Loba and Margret. If Sparks examined them, surely some medical evidence would show up.

In the meantime, she had several hours to kill. Jas lay on her bunk and turned on her screen to access the ship's massive database. She stroked the image displayed, scrolling through the long list of options, until she found the section she was looking for: Hostile Extraterrestrial Life Forms.

Each species was cataloged under its Earth name in phonetic script. She'd logged a few of these dangerous aliens herself. Though humans had never encountered a species that posed a threat outside its own planet, there seemed to be plenty of nasties lying in wait for unsuspecting prospectors on new worlds. Many of the more recent additions were unfamiliar to Jas. She clicked on a promising link on surprise attacks. It was a passage on long, lithe, ground-dwelling organisms that burrowed up from the dirt and into the feet of animals walking overhead. The creatures quickly tunneled through flesh and bones and into the main body, drawn to the central nervous system, which they then devoured.

Jas recalled the news of the life form's discovery. It couldn't penetrate combat suits, and neither the C.S.O. leading the LIV nor his defense units had felt or taken note of the small thumps against the soles of their boots. The

C.S.O. had given the planet the all-clear. The organisms had quickly massacred the first RA team to land. Had the team been wearing combat suits, they would have been fine, but, despite their own massive salaries, Polestar Corp's executive board had judged the provision of combat suits for RA teams to be too expensive.

Jas scrolled on. Previously unknown intelligent life—or, more correctly, life that Polestar acknowledged as intelligent, despite the obvious disincentive— was rare, but hostile life was common. The role of chief security officer was nigh on impossible to perform well. What new horrors a planet might hold were highly unpredictable, yet after a few short LIVs, security officers were expected to clear the areas as safe for resource assessment. Though their contracts stated that they carried no personal liability if they made a mistake, the emotional toll of seeing friends and colleagues die because they made a bad call could be devastating.

Jas counted herself lucky that, so far, no one had died on her watch, though she'd had some close calls. She couldn't do her job properly with Loba tying her hands. It was poetic justice that it looked like the master himself had fallen victim to his own lax expediency.

She filtered the information in the database for parasites, body possession, mind control, and influence on human behavior. The results dwindled to a handful. The only case she could find that sounded similar to what was happening on K. 67092d was an incident involving a gas in a planet's atmosphere that scanners had failed to detect. The security officer in that case couldn't be blamed for what had happened. Wearing his combat suit, he hadn't breathed the local air. It wasn't part of the job. Scientists were the testers. Security officers weren't canaries in coalmines, and defense units don't breath. When the RA team had arrived, the gas had entered their bloodstreams and crossed the blood-brain barrier. It'd destroyed their higher brain functions, and the team had been reduced to living, breathing vegetables within minutes.

She closed the database screen, and rested her arm over her eyes. Despite these terrible accidents, people continued to sign up for work aboard the prospecting ships. Life on Earth grew harder every year, and the chances of achieving a financially comfortable, long life and peaceful retirement grew slimmer. Jas understood only too well why companies like Polestar had an endless queue of applicants. The get-rich-quick prospect was tantalizing to many, and employers downplayed the risks. How long would her lucky streak of protecting these crews last? Maybe it was time for her to consider another career.

Her interface chirruped. She had a message from Sparks. Reading it, she groaned. She'd failed the mental health assessment. Of course. The doctor prescribed a muscle relaxant, an anti-psychotic, and an anti-anxiety medication. He was going to dope her up as revenge for her forceful eviction of him from her cabin. She thumped the wall with her fist so hard she hurt her hand. *Damn the misborn.* But she couldn't refuse treatment. Loba—or whatever was now controlling him—could have her put in the brig, where there would be no way to sneak out. If she was restrained indefinitely, for the rest of the mission, who would protect the crew? She grimaced. She hadn't been doing that great a job of protecting them herself.

She turned on her side. She had to think of a plan, but nothing would come. After some time, mental exhaustion forced her eyes closed, and she slept.

She was back in Antarctica. It was summer, and the ice was melting. The ground was slick and treacherous. Soon, there would be no ice left, they said. Great sheets had broken off over the previous few decades, floating away to slowly melt into the ocean. Billions of tons of fresh water ice, gone forever.

Jas was looking out over the ocean. At first, she couldn't remember why she was there, then it came to her. She was looking for something. She'd lost something in the water, and she had to find it.

She rolled up her pants legs and took off her boots and socks. The first touch of the icy water on her toes made her suck in a breath. She waded deeper, and the waves soon soaked her pants up to her thighs and numbed her feet and calves. What was she looking for? She couldn't remember, except that it was something important. A sense of urgency rose up in her. She went deeper in, up to her waist. She had to find it quickly, or it would be too late. A wave took her full in the face, and she choked on seawater.

Something heavy bumped against her thigh. Was this it? She grabbed blindly in the water. Her fingers met cloth. She took hold of it and pulled. This was it. Finally, she'd found it.

A face rose up: skin deathly pale, eyes open and still, mouth spilling water, black hair trailing. Jas tried to scream, but another wave took her, ripping the man from her grasp. It lifted her from her feet, and crushed her under its weight. She couldn't breathe. She fought to reach the surface, but she was trapped in the rolling water. She was going to drown, she was—gasping, awakening.

Jas sat upright in her bunk. It took her a few moments to realize where she was, that she wasn't back at training college in Antarctica, and that it had all been a dream. The same nightmare as always.

She lay down and, after some time, she slept.

Her door chime woke her. Groggy with sleep, for a tense moment Jas thought Loba or Margret had come to take her to the planet so she could be possessed by an alien. She sat up, trying to figure out who was at the door. Was it a drone with Spark's prescription? No, the pills had been put through her door slot. Her memory fully returned. She'd asked Lingiari to come over. "Door, open."

The rangy copilot stood in the entrance, clutching a box and looking pleased, for some reason. Maybe he'd figured out what they should do.

"Come in," said Jas. "What's been happening? How are Margret and Loba acting? Has anyone else been affected?"

"Woah, slow down," said Lingiari. "Have you eaten? Are you hungry?" He sat down and put the box on her desk. He began to open it.

"No, I'm not," replied Jas, though her stomach rumbled as she spoke. *What was the man doing? Didn't he understand the situation?* The copilot was peeling the lid off a foil pack. A rich, fishy scent escaped, and Jas's mouth watered. "Tell me what happened on the RA trip today. What did you see?"

"Eat up, and I'll tell you all about it." He held out the package and a fork. "It's smoked oysters."

"Lingiari, I don't know what the hell you're doing, but, please, cut it out and answer me."

The man seemed to deflate. He took back the oysters, sighed, and started to eat them himself. "What do you want to know?" He spoke from the corner of his mouth as he chewed. "I took a team down for an RA and brought them back when they'd finished. That's it."

"Where did they go? Did they enter one of the structures? Were they acting strangely like Loba and Margret when they came back?"

Lingiari swallowed and licked his fork before plunging it into the oysters again. "They weren't near any buildings this time. It was a volcanic zone. Pretty active. Had to get out when the ship's scanners detected that a potential earthquake was building."

"That's a relief. It sounds like the RA team was safe this time, but we've got to do something, Lingiari. If we don't, the whole crew's in danger."

The copilot's attention was on a large forkful of pale brown oysters on its way to his mouth, dripping oil. "Yeah, but..." he popped the oysters in and looked thoughtful as his mouth worked, "what?"

"We need to convince the other officers that Loba isn't to be trusted, and they'll declare him incompetent and take over the running of the ship. They'll get us away from this planet. Sparks can try to find out what's happened to the master and Margret. I might be able to convince them if you back me up. They must have noticed that Loba's acting oddly by now."

"Take over the running of the *Galathea*?" Carl put down his fork. "Isn't that mutiny?"

"Not if the master's incapacitated, it isn't. It's the only sensible thing the officers can do. I just need to persuade them. You'll support me, right?"

"I'm right by your side, Jas. Can I call you Jas, Harrington? I'm with you. In everything." He gazed into her eyes.

"Great," replied Jas, wondering briefly if Lingiari had been infected too. But he wasn't acting vacant like Loba and Margret. Just...peculiar. "In that case, you can come with me."

"What? Where are you going?"

"Where do you think I'm going? The bridge. And you're coming with me." She jumped up and strode past Lingiari. The copilot hastily pushed his fork into the tin of oysters, but it slipped out and fell to the floor with a clatter.

"Don't you think you're being a bit quick off the mark?" he asked. But Jas was already on her way out.

12

Her mind was made up, and Jas acted. She sped through the *Galathea* toward the bridge, where Loba and other high-ranking staff could be found when they were on shift. From behind her came the sound of Lingiari'ss footsteps, half-running to keep up.

"Harrington, hey, slow down."

A crew member gaped as he recognized her. The news that she'd been confined to her cabin must have been hot gossip around the ship. She brushed past him, nearly knocking the man from his feet.

"Wait a minute, Harrington," the copilot called.

"We don't have time for any more talking, Lingiari," she said over her shoulder. "Every RA team that goes down to the planet is vulnerable. We know Margret and Loba have been infected. How many more are there? We have to convince the officers about what's happening and get them to call a halt to the assessment trips."

Lingiari caught up with her and grabbed her arm. "You know, on second thoughts, I don't think this is such a good idea."

Jas stopped and faced him. "Do you have a better one?" They were in a high-traffic corridor. *Galathea* crew members passed on either side, giving the pair looks. One woman paused at the sight of them and moved a short distance away before speaking into her comm button. When Lingiari didn't answer her question, Jas said, "I have to get to the bridge, now. Before it's too late."

She strode away without checking if Lingiari was following. If he wasn't going to support her, she would just have to try her best by herself. A moment later, she burst into the flight control room. All eyes turned to her as she stood at the door.

Jas rarely went to the bridge, but the oval area was just as she remembered it. Displayed on the walls around the room were images of the star systems and planets scheduled for investigation and assessment that mission. Below the planets that they had already assessed was a set of figures estimating their resource availability and potential revenue. The figures were red. When the *Galathea* claimed sufficient resources to bring in bonuses, the numbers below the planets would be green. The display had been Loba's idea, to keep everyone's mind on the money. It was a constant reminder to the officers to work faster and harder.

The master was in his usual spot, seated on an elevated plinth toward the back of the room. First Mate Haggardy was to one side, reading an interface. The second mate's seat on the other side of Loba was empty, but the rest of them— the chief engineer, third mate, pilot, quartermaster, RA team leader and a handful of cadets—were at their stations. Navigator Lee was looking at her with her mouth open.

For a moment, no one spoke. Now that she was there, Jas wasn't sure what to say; how could she convince them that their master was compromised, with Loba sitting right there looking exactly the same as always? But couldn't they see there was something wrong? He should have reacted strongly to her presence. He should have commanded her removal. But he only stared like the rest of them. Couldn't they tell, or were they too afraid of being the first to say something?

Haggardy was the first to act. He pressed the comm link on his desk. "Security to the bridge." His eyes narrowed at her. "You're disobeying orders, Harrington. You heard what the master said. If you leave your cabin, you're to be sent to the brig."

"Wait, listen to me. Loba went planetside with Margret Stratton. You know that. They've been taken over by something on the planet. I don't know what it is, but you have to halt the RA trips before we have more victims. The master isn't fit to serve and should be removed from duty."

"Dr. Sparks forwarded your report," said Haggardy. "You're suffering from a mental illness. These thoughts you're having are just one of your symptoms."

"I'm not sick," Jas exclaimed. She pointed at Loba. "Haven't you noticed he's been acting strangely?"

Haggardy turned to Loba, who only returned the gaze and shook his head slightly. "Stop right there, Harrington," Haggardy said. "I don't care how ill you are. I won't have you accusing the master of this vessel of incompetency."

"What about that trip he took, Haggardy? Any of you?" She scanned their faces. From their expressions, she wasn't convincing anyone. She clenched her fists. "When has he ever done anything like that? Look at him. He's been acting weird since, hasn't he?" No one would meet her eyes. Lingiari had come in with her, but he was hanging in the background, looking non-committal. "Lingiari agrees with me," she blurted.

"That's enough," said Haggardy. "Don't start dragging other crew members into your fantasy."

The bridge door opened, and Jas turned to see two on-ship security officers enter. *Her* officers. They looked embarrassed and a little afraid.

"Take her to the brig," commanded Haggardy.

Jas swung back to face him. "I'm not going anywhere until you listen to me. You cannot leave that man in charge of the ship. You have to stop the crew from going down to the planet."

Haggardy motioned with his head to the security detail behind her. Hands gripped her arms. The situation was getting annoying. She back-fisted one man, breaking his nose, and drove her elbow into the solar plexus of the other. As the men staggered back, she turned and kicked the head of the man holding his stomach. He fell down senseless. The one whose nose she'd broken drew his weapon. Blood dripped from his chin, and his eyes watered.

Jas put her hands on her hips. "Frank, really?"

Frank quailed under her stare, and in his momentary distraction, Jas kicked the weapon from his hand and moved in for a headlock. "Sorry," she said, as she knocked his skull just hard enough against a rail that he dropped, unconscious, to the floor. She would have to improve training for on-ship security. That was much too easy. They'd gotten slack. Jas scooped up the fallen weapon and took the other man's from its holster. "Thanks, Haggardy. Now you have to listen to me." She swept the room with the weapons. Lingiari had backed into a corner. "Just go," Jas told him.

As the copilot left, Jas began to outline to the flight control room what they had to do. Loba, Margret, and everyone else who had been to the planet without the protection of a combat suit—there had to be a reason she was unaffected, despite entering the structures—was under suspicion and had to be relieved of duty while they were tested. All RA trips had to be cancelled, and the *Galathea* would have to return to Earth and enter quarantine while the xenobiologists figured out what to do.

While she was speaking the assembled officers and cadets remained silent. She stopped. There was an uncomfortable pause. To her surprise, Haggardy said, "Maybe you have a point there, Harrington. Tell us some more." He glanced at the door. He must have called another security detail while she was distracted with dealing with the first one. *Damn the misborn.* She'd have to fight these officers too. It didn't matter. She could take down any of her on-ship guards. Being better than them was part of her job. Eventually, Haggardy and the others would have to listen to her.

The two men she'd knocked out were coming around. She trained her weapons on their figures. Behind them, the bridge door opened, and Jas's jaw dropped. *Krat.* Haggardy hadn't called on-ship security, he'd summoned two of her defense units. AX7 and AX10 lumbered onto the deck. There would be no defeating these two. No intimidation nor recourse to personal history. Defense units obeyed the highest-ranking officer's commands unquestioningly and unrelentingly. Taking her to the brig was just another task for them.

At least they hadn't activated their weapons yet.

Her only chance was to disable them quickly. At close range, she might manage it. She knew where they were most vulnerable. Jas lifted her laser guns and took aim, but her fingers wouldn't press the triggers. She couldn't fire on them, even though she knew they would eventually self-repair. She couldn't bring herself to damage these part-organic machines. Whatever injuries she inflicted, the units would do whatever Haggardy commanded with no regard for their own safety.

They came toward her. She held her weapons steady. She had to shoot. She had to put them out of action, but still her fingers froze. It wasn't the expense that bothered her, nor the fact that they were two amazingly intricate, complex items of equipment. It was her long experience of working with them. She'd gotten to know every facet of their behavior, including all the little quirks and individualities they weren't supposed to have.

The idea of harming either of the units turned her stomach. She threw down the weapons.

"Fine," she exclaimed, turning back to Haggardy. "Put me in the brig. And when you see I was right, that he's possessed," she stabbed a finger at Loba, "come and get me to help you sort out this mess."

AX10 and AX7 took her by the arms and pulled her toward the door.

"The rest of you: do not go down to the planet. Do you hear me? There's something in those structures. Don't set a foot down on the planet. And watch anyone who does."

13

Sayen Lee was sleeping restlessly when stomach pangs brought her to full consciousness. She needed a physician. Though it was the quiet shift, she didn't think Dr. Sparks would mind seeing her. He was always so obliging. In a short time, she was at his desk.

"Navigator Lee, how pleasant to see you again. Please take a seat." Sparks smiled widely and gestured to the chair opposite him.

Just seeing the man made Sayen feel better. She loved the way he'd set up his consulting room like the physicians' offices of the twenty-first century. There were none of the bulky scanners and equipment that now filled health clinics to the brim: machines to analyze the breath, upright full-body scanners, equipment to extract and test blood. He had these devices and more, but he hid them away in the back, out of sight. She'd even heard there was now a machine to perform gynaecological exams. She gave a slight shudder.

Sparks put his elbows on his desk, steepled his fingers, and gazed into Sayen's eyes. "And what can I do for you today?"

This was what she liked most. Sparks made an effort to talk to his patients. She put a hand on her stomach. "I've been feeling queasy ever since breakfast yesterday, Doctor. I think I might be coming down with something. Or maybe it was something I ate."

"Hmmm, I see." He turned to a screen and typed into a keyboard. "Any other symptoms? Changes to your bowel habits? Have you vomited at all?"

"No, that's it. But I did feel worse after that incident with Harrington on the bridge. So maybe it's something to do with my nerves?"

"That was very unfortunate. Very sad." Sparks shook his head. "If only she'd taken the medication I prescribed." He stopped typing and leaned toward the navigator. "I probably shouldn't say anything," he said, lowering his voice, "but she's a natural, you know. Means she's a little unstable." He tapped the side of his head.

Sayen's eyes grew wide. "Is that right? I didn't know. That naturals have worse mental health, I mean."

"That's only the start of it. They're more vulnerable to most medical conditions, which is why it's helpful for me to know who's who among the crew, if you know what I mean. But the powers that be have tied my hands in that regard, I'm sorry to say." He paused. "But that isn't you're problem, is it, Navigator?"

Sayen gave a short laugh. "No, my parents paid for the works for me and my brother." She frowned. "And yet, I seem to get sick all the time. Why is that, I wonder?"

"Hmmm, well..." Sparks scanned his screen. "As I've said before, your profile indicates a strong immune response to viruses, so you can thank your modding for that. I suppose it's possible that when you come into contact with a virus, your immune system's reaction is excessive. Many symptoms of infection are in fact due to the chemicals the body produces as a response to pathogens. When someone with a weaker response fights off a virus, they might not notice, but *your* body's mounting a full-out attack, and you're feeling it."

"Uh-huh. That makes sense."

"But let's be thorough about this, hm? Hop up on the couch, and I'll examine you."

A pleasant warmth suffused Sayen. Dr. Sparks always took her concerns seriously. She climbed onto his examining table and pulled up her tunic, exposing her midriff. The doctor rubbed his hands together as he approached the table. "Wouldn't want to shock you with my cold hands." He placed his open palms on her bare skin and gently pushed, palpating her internal organs. Sayen's tummy gurgled, and she giggled.

"Nothing to be embarrassed about. It's a good sign, in fact," said the doctor. "Indicates everything's working normally."

"Thanks, Doctor. I already feel a little better."

"Good, good," said Sparks. "You can get up now." He returned to his desk. Typing on his keyboard as Sayen got down from the table, he added, "I can't find anything abnormal. I think it's just a case of a little anxiety, especially as you say the problem got worse after witnessing our chief security officer's outburst today. I'm going to prescribe a medication that will calm your stomach."

"Thank you, Doctor." Her comm button chirruped. "Excuse me." She clicked on the Polestar symbol fixed to her chest and lifted it up to read the message. It was from Loba. *Navigator Lee, report to the shuttle bay.* Sayen froze.

"Is something the matter?" asked Sparks.

"I think...I think...Master Loba wants me to go down to the planet." There was no other reason she could think of that would require her presence in the shuttle bay in the middle of the quiet shift. Harrington's warnings echoed in her head. Her mind whirled.

"That'll be a nice trip for you. I often wish I had more of an opportunity for exploring new planets, but my duties nearly always confine me to the ship."

"I always stay aboard the ship. Always," Sayen blurted.

"Now's your chance then. I envy you." Sparks pressed a final key on his keyboard and turned to her, smiling. "I'll have a drone drop your medication at your cabin. It'll be there in ten or fifteen minutes."

Her consultation was over, but Sayen didn't want to leave. "Dr. Sparks...Harrington, before she was taken to the brig, she said that the master had been infected by an alien, and she warned us not to go to the planet, and now..."

The doctor smiled. "C.S.O. Harrington is suffering from a mental illness. You shouldn't take any notice of what she said. I'm sure there's nothing to fear."

"But it's strange Loba would command that, right after Harrington said—"

"Navigator Lee, I'm surprised. I never thought you would be the type to question the master's orders. Perhaps you've been spending a little too much time around C.S.O Harrington."

Sparks's smile was gone. He was watching her. She had no choice but to leave. All concerns about her minor stomach complaint were gone from her mind. She did not want to go planetside, whether Harrington was right or not. She had to think of a way to avoid the order.

First, she headed in the direction of her cabin, but it occurred to her that Loba would send someone to look for her if she didn't show up at the shuttle bay, and then she would have no choice but to obey the order. Her heart raced.

She needed to stop panicking and think. Turning on her heel, she headed toward a different part of the ship. She would have to find somewhere to hide. Her comm chirruped. Another message. *Navigator Lee, you are expected at the shuttle bay. Please report immediately.*

Her throat was tight. *Don't set a foot down there,* Harrington had said. Had Loba been taken over by an alien? Was he trying to get her infected too? It made sense. The navigator was essential to the ship's operation. Programming starjumps incorrectly could be disastrous. If the aliens wanted the *Galathea* under their control, they needed her.

She imagined another creature possessing her, and her skin crawled. She began to run. She had to find somewhere to get away from Loba...and Margret! Her odd behavior suddenly made sense. The geo-phys scientist had been taken over too, just as Harrington had said.

Sayen tried to think of a good hiding place. Where would no one think to look? She jogged along the corridors, attracting glances from the few crew members she passed. Her comm chirruped again. She didn't answer the call. Remembering the button held a tracker, she pulled it off and tossed it to the floor. That would delay them a bit.

Her pulse was racing. Flashbacks from her childhood ran through her mind. Memories of playing hide-and-seek in her large family home. Driven indoors by midday temperatures, she and her brother had been forced to play quietly to avoid bothering their parents, who both worked from home.

Three years older, her brother had always been better at hiding than her. She would spend hours wandering the house in frustrated searches. At the time, he'd been careful to never give away his secrets. It had taken years before he'd admitted he'd been hiding above doorways, perched with one foot on the open door and the other on the doorframe. He'd also hidden spread-eagled under covers to make the bed look empty.

She was panting now. Once her comm button was found, they would know she was on the run. Then they would put out a ship wide—

"Navigator Lee, report to the shuttle bay immediately, on pain of disciplinary action," came the ship's synthesized voice over the corridor intercom. "All crew members, please conduct a search for Navigator Lee and report her whereabouts to Master Loba directly."

Krat.

She was in a residential section of the ship. The corridor was empty for now, but her luck wouldn't hold for long. She had another childhood flashback. Her brother's best strategy, his last confession when their hide-and-seek days were long over, was that he'd never stayed in one place. He would move into areas she'd already searched, and the first hiding place he'd used was her own room.

Margret's cabin! Margret had been possessed. She would be out searching for her. Her cabin would be the last place she'd look.

14

Disabling Margret's door lock took a matter of moments. Polestar's on-ship security systems were cheap and easily circumvented by someone who, as a child, had delighted in taking apart any computer that strayed under her fingers. The door slid open, and Sayen went inside. Silently, the door closed behind her. Looking around the familiar room, Sayen thought of Margret, and wondered what the alien had done to her. Was she conscious of being possessed, but unable to do anything about it? She suddenly felt chilled.

It looked like Harrington wasn't mentally ill. She'd been right all along. Sayen wished she'd done more to support the security chief, but the woman had acted so angry and wild. If she'd stayed calm and explained properly, Sayen would have listened. Now that she'd gotten herself locked up in the brig, who was going to save them?

She sat on Margret's bunk and popped her knuckles as she considered what to do. Darn but that woman was messy. The bunk was unmade. She stood up and paced the cabin. It was only a matter of time before she was found. She had to do something to stop the possessed Loba, but did she have to act alone? Sayen recalled that the copilot, Lingiari, had come onto the bridge with Harrington. He must have known what was going on, too. She had to find him, but she couldn't use the comm system. Her messages could be picked up and traced. What to do? She paced some more. She couldn't figure out how to find Lingiari without getting caught. Maybe Loba was already forcing him to fly to the planet.

There was a soft knock at the door. Her heart stopped. Had she been found, or was someone looking for Margret? But who would knock instead of using the door chime? She went to the viewer, and her stomach dropped when she saw who it was. The copilot. What the hell was he doing there? She thumbed the intercom. "Lingiari?" she whispered.

"Lee, open up."

She did as he asked, and, glancing from side to side, the copilot slipped into the room.

"What the hell are you doing here?" asked Sayen. "How did you find me?"

Lingiari reached up to the wall vent and pulled off the cover. A winged creature climbed out and walked up his arm and onto his shoulder, where it sat like a pirate captain's parrot. "This is my mate, Flux. I asked him to look for officers who had disobeyed Loba's order and were hiding out. He flies around the aeration system for exercise. Knows the ship like the back of his wing."

"But...you can't have an animal aboard ship," spluttered Sayen. "Especially not an alien animal. It's against regulations."

"Yeah, but it's no big deal, right? And, believe me, if it weren't for Flux here, the cockroach problem would be a lot worse. Isn't that right, mate?"

Flux waggled his ears in reply.

Sayen was flummoxed and a little alarmed by the presence of the alien, but they didn't have time to waste in further discussion about it. "What's happening, Lingiari? Loba was ordering me to go to the shuttle bay. Is he going planetside, and how come you aren't taking him?"

"I was supposed to be taking him. Him and everyone who was ordered to the shuttle bay. We all got comm'd about the same time. It was me and the senior officers. Some of them went, but the rest had seen or heard about what Harrington'd said, and they wouldn't go. They were standing around outside their cabins in the officers' section, trying to figure out what to do. Where were you?"

"I got the same comm, but I was on the other side of the ship seeing Dr. Sparks."

"Lucky for you. Loba called in the defense units, or whatever's possessing him did. He must've figured it out after he saw Haggardy order them to take Harrington to the brig."

"He used defense units to round the officers up?"

"Pretty much. Nothing they could do. No one was armed. Caught them by surprise. I only got away because I had a bit of a head start, thanks to Harrington. I was out of sight of the rest when I heard the units running up and the officers shouting."

"This is a disaster," said Sayen. "Did anyone try to stop Loba?"

"As far as I could tell, he left it all to the units. He wasn't there, and anyway, it all happened too fast. You've seen them fellas. No one's going to try tackling a defense unit. It would only have taken a few of them to do the job."

"Where are the rest, do you think?"

"Waiting for Loba's orders, probably."

Sayen sat on Margret's bunk. She had a sudden, insane urge to tidy the cabin up and clean every inch of it. She put her head in her hands. This wasn't supposed to be happening. If she'd wanted a dangerous job, she would have joined the military. "What now?"

"Dunno, but I'm guessing the units got most of the senior officers to the shuttle bay, and since Loba doesn't know where I am, he's going to make Grantwise fly them planetside."

Resting her forehead on her fingertips, Sayen frowned. She looked up at the copilot. "What if we tell the rest of the crew what's happened? We could get control of the *Galathea* while Loba's planetside with the officers."

"It'll be hard. The officers got taken fast, when most of the crew was asleep. I don't know if anyone saw anything. We'd be asking them to commit mutiny just because of something we told them. Why should they believe us? No one's going to bang on Loba's door in the middle of the quiet shift to check he's there." The copilot sat next to Sayen. His pet was still sitting on his shoulder. Flux leaned across to Sayen's head and began to delicately inspect her hair, pulling it apart with his wing hooks.

The navigator twisted her head away from the animal's reach, grimacing. "Lingiari, tell your animal to leave me alone."

"Sorry," said Flux, "I was just checking for parasites."

"It can talk? Ough, I hate these modded animals." She scooted to the far end of the bunk. "And I *don't* have parasites."

"I'm not modded, and I'd appreciate it if you didn't talk about me like I'm not here." Flux climbed down from Lingiari's shoulder and slipped into a gap in his shirt, in an apparent sulk.

"Never mind, mate," the copilot murmured in the direction of his chest. "I know you mean well."

"Mutiny," Sayen said, as if it were the first time she'd heard the word. What a pair of mutineers they made. She, small and bookish; he, a lanky second-best pilot. But they were all they had. Or were they? "Hey, we're forgetting something. Loba's trip in the shuttle will give us some time. Maybe enough time to spring Harrington from the brig."

Lingiari's face brightened, but then he said, "How're we gonna do that? Security's tighter than a gnat's arse over there."

"You're forgetting some things. One, I'm an expert on the ship's computer."

"And what's the other thing?"

"Not thing, things."

15

Carl couldn't believe what he was about to do. It seemed impossible, but Lee had seemed convinced it would work, and it made sense, yet... He surveyed the defense units that remained on the ship, standing in a row in their storage room in the half-light. What if they ignored his command? Or worse, what if they attacked him? He was conscious of the soft warmth of Flux's body against his chest. He'd tried to persuade the animal to return to his cabin for safety, but he'd refused. There was no reasoning with him when he was in a sulk.

Carl took a breath. He could do this. "Defense units..." His voice petered out as the huge, identical heads turned to him with blank stares. The androids had always given him the willies. The only thing human about them, in his experience, was the way they looked. He'd always tried to avoid them as much as he could. "Defense units, arm yourselves...?" It was a simple request. A test to see if Lee was— He exhaled as the units' thick forearms opened and weapons slid into their hands. The navigator was right.

They really would obey him in the absence of orders from a higher-ranking officer.

In a stronger tone, he continued, "Follow me to the brig." He waited, but the units didn't move. *Krat.* Had he said it wrong? "Defense units, follow me to the brig." Still no reaction. Then he realized what was wrong. He was an idiot. He'd told them to follow him, but he wasn't going anywhere. They were waiting for him to leave. Carl went into the ship's corridor, watching the units as he walked. They immediately left the room and came up behind him.

He led the way, and the units followed in single file, exactly equidistant from each other, weapons held at an identical angle. After a short while, Carl grew bolder. "Units, double-time to the brig," he barked. He was forced to leap out of the way as they ran toward him, threatening to run him down. He sped after them as they drew away. So his *follow me* order had been superseded by the next order. Commanding the massive androids wasn't straightforward.

At the brig, the guards didn't seem to have noticed that Lee had remotely inactivated the locks when Carl and the defense units arrived. They must have been alerted by the thumps of the units' feet, however, for the two of them had run forward and were gripping their weapons and looking nervous as the units turned into the corridor. Carl stayed well back. He'd given the defense units their orders and was going to let them do their job without interference.

The guards' eyes widened and their mouths grew to Os at the sight of the towering androids bearing down on them. One froze entirely. The other snapped out of his trance long enough to lower his weapon, take aim, and fire at a unit. He hit it dead center, and the unit fell back, smoking from a hole in its chest. Carl winced. Harrington wasn't going to like that. Everyone knew how protective she was of them.

One shot was all the guard had time for before the rest were upon him and his partner. True to Carl's instructions, they were careful not to hurt them. Their weapons were for intimidation only. The units didn't even stun the guards, only disarmed and restrained them.

"Lingiari," said a guard as Carl approached. "What the hell are you doing?" A defense unit stood behind him, holding him in a bear hug. The guard's face was pink with exertion as he struggled to free himself.

"Sorry, but I've gotta get Harrington out," replied Carl. "An alien's controlling Loba, and it's trying to take over the ship. He's ordered the officers onto the shuttle and taken them planetside. We're going to stop them from docking when they get back, or something, I don't know. But we need Harrington."

"Krat," said the guard, ceasing his struggles. "That's news to me. I tell you what, order this misborn to let me go, and I'll help you."

"I don't know about that."

"Come on, man. Seriously, I thought there was something up. Harrington's been telling us all about it. She wouldn't stop going on about how Loba wasn't to be trusted. I didn't believe her. Sounded like BF, but if you're saying it too, I'm right with you. Come on. You're going to need all the crew you can get."

"Hmmm...okay," Carl said. He looked at the unit holding the guard. "Let him go." When the android didn't respond, he reframed his command. "AX..." he peered at the unit's breastplate, "...5, let go of the man you're holding."

The minute he was free, the guard stooped to pick up his weapon and lifted the barrel to aim it at Carl. A blow from the fist of the unit who had been holding him struck the side of his head, and he fell to the floor unconscious.

"Err...thanks," said Carl. "AX5, could you—"

"Affirmative. I will restrain him, copilot Lingiari."

Carl left behind the units and guards at the brig entrance and slid the unlocked door into the wall. It was reinforced plexisteel, but useless against Navigator Lee's infiltration into the ship's control center. The copilot wondered where she'd gone to gain access to the computer. Inside the brig were four cells, two on either side of the corridor, large enough to hold twenty or so people. The walls between the cells and the corridor were checkerboards of opaque and transparent cubes. All the cells were empty but one.

Jas Harrington's face was pressed against a transparent cube, which distorted her nose somewhat. Carl thought she still looked great.

"Lingiari?"

"Call me Carl, hey?" he said in a rush of excitement and pride. This must be how it felt to be a hero. "Come out, Jas. It's open. Your door's unlocked. Lee's deactivated every lock in the place."

Harrington pushed the door and looked at it wonderingly as it opened. "I didn't hear a thing. How...?"

"Dunno. I'm just doing the grunt work. We had to get you out. Loba's got most of the officers on the shuttle, and he's taken them planetside."

The chief security officer's expression was grim as she stepped into the corridor and moved toward him. Carl half-lifted his arms toward her. Jas gave him a puzzled glance as she passed him on her way to the exit, saying, "What happened to the guards? And what's that lump in your shirt?"

Carl's arms dropped to his sides, disappointedly. He followed her. "Your defense units took the guards out."

Harrington spun to face him. "What? How come? What did you do?"

"Lee said they're programmed to obey the orders of the highest ranking officer. So I went and...what?" Harrington's expression was unnerving him.

"You commanded my units?"

"You say that like it's a bad thing. What did you want me to do? We had to get you out somehow."

"Did any of them get hurt?"

"One of them got...one of them got a bit singed."

Harrington ran the rest of the way to the entrance of the brig, where the defense units were still restraining the guards. The guard who had been knocked out was coming around. The unit was holding him upright. His head was slumped forward, but it lifted as Harrington approached. His eyes immediately sought his weapon, but it had been kicked well out of his reach.

"You'll regret this, Harrington," he said. "You never were mentally ill, were you? I know what this is. It's mutiny. But you won't get away with it. We'll hunt you down, and when we get back to Earth you're going to jail."

Ignoring the guard, Harrington went straight to the defense unit who had been hit. Carl followed her. The unit had retreated down the corridor and around a corner, and it was standing motionless, a wisp of smoke eddying up from its chest wound.

"Why are you always the one that gets hit? AX7, damage report."

"Grade 5 internal damage affecting temperature regulation, gross motor control, and energy distribution, C.S.O. Harrington. Injury repair initiated."

"Can you make it back to storage by yourself?"

"Affirmative, C.S.O. Harrington."

"Return and repair."

The defense unit obeyed. Harrington went back to the guards. "You're lucky I don't know which one of you shot my unit." She sighed and passed a hand over her eyes. "I know how this looks, but believe me, there's something on that planet that's got control of Loba. He isn't himself. I'm going to find out what it is and destroy it, and then we're getting out of here. If you've got any sense, you would avoid the master and the officers as best you can. And, whatever you do, don't go down to the planet, even if it means disobeying a direct order."

She addressed the units holding the guards. "AX5 and AX10, put these men in the brig, secure the doors, and return to storage. All other defense units, return to storage now. Let's go," she said to Lingiari.

After they were out of hearing range of the guards, she asked, "What are we going to do?"

"Me and Lee kinda hoped you would know," Carl replied.

16

First Mate Jack Haggardy rubbed his graying stubble. Around him, in the passenger cabin of the shuttle, sat most of the *Galathea's* officers. Eight defense units stood at the edges of the cabin, as many as the space accommodated. The rest of them had been left behind on the ship. The units were unseated, and their weapons were fixed on the officers. No one was speaking.

Haggardy certainly wasn't going to attract any attention. Not rocking the boat had been his MO for his entire career aboard prospecting ships, and it had served him well. Always following orders to the letter, no matter what, never gainsaying superior officers in public or private, never back-stabbing, being constantly congenial and easy to work with, and so on. He was no one's enemy, and everyone thought him their friend. Over time, Haggardy had risen steadily through the ranks.

It didn't bother him that he'd never made master. A master's bonuses were attractive but not worth the additional responsibility. First mate was as high as you could go while still being able to pass the buck when a mission was unsuccessful, or people died, or if there was a governmental inquiry into claiming a planet inhabited by an intelligent species. Making first mate but not master was, in Haggardy's opinion, a great success. The current mission was supposed to have been the final one before his retirement.

But this latest turn of events had put everything in jeopardy.

Judging from the looks on the other officers' faces, they were shocked and scared, but none of them seemed to be up to saying or doing anything. Haggardy was not going to be the first to resist. He'd seen people ruin their careers or even die that way. Let others take the risk. He had too much to lose.

Stealing a glance at Loba from the corners of his eyes, he noted that the man's face was expressionless. The geo-phys woman sitting next to the master looked the same. Though he hated to admit it, there was clearly more than a little truth to what Harrington had been harping on about. Physically, the master was unchanged, as far as Haggardy could tell, but his behavior was unfathomable. He'd offered no explanation for the trip to the planet, and his use of the defense units to force the officers to comply was barbaric.

So, Loba and the scientist were possessed by aliens. Haggardy had heard of stranger things in his long career. Reluctant though he was to act, if he didn't do something to save himself, he would end up the same.

If only he'd paid heed to Harrington's warning not to go to the planet. He'd been taken by surprise as he was relaxing in his cabin, and before he knew it, he was forced into the shuttle. But maybe the security officer had said something else that would help him. He frowned as he tried to remember her rant, which he hadn't paid much attention to at the time. She'd mentioned something about the structures on the surface. They had something to do with it. He had to try to avoid going into them.

"Haggardy," murmured Javek, the resource assessment chief, in the next seat. Haggardy could barely hear her. Her voice was so low, in fact, that he felt confident in ignoring her as if he hadn't heard her speak. But he couldn't possibly ignore the elbow Javek thrust in his side a few moments later. He stifled a grunt. Loba glanced in his direction, but he failed to locate the source of the noise. The master returned to staring ahead.

"This is madness," continued Javek. "What are you going to do?"

"I don't know what you mean."

"Don't be ridiculous. Loba's been infested by something, just like Harrington said. You have to do something about it. You're first mate, next in command. It's your responsibility."

"We must follow the master's orders. Failure to do so is cause for dismissal and—" He sucked in a breath as Loba turned and stared directly at him. Haggardy clamped his lips together.

He didn't speak again for the rest of the trip. His thoughts were focused on how to avoid entering the structures on the planet when they landed. Perhaps he could get away somehow while the others were forced in, but he couldn't think up a plan.

Touchdown was heavy. The shuttle bounced when it hit the ground, eliciting gasps and a few small screams from the terrified passengers. The ship's pilot, Grantwise, was clearly out of practice with small ships.

Loba commanded the officers to leave the vessel, and under the threatening weapons of the defense units, they silently obeyed. The scene was dreamlike. The officers knew they were going to a terrible fate, yet none of them seemed able to do anything to prevent it. Haggardy was reminded of a herd of cattle walking obediently to the slaughterhouse.

A keen, cold wind swept his long hair into his eyes as he reached the bottom of the shuttle's ramp. He brushed the hair away and saw that among the uneven scrub of the planet surface, one of the structures sat ominously near. If he was going to do something, it had to be soon.

It was another officer who broke first. Javek.

"Sir," she exclaimed, her cheeks flaming red. The master stopped. He was at the front of the line that had been threading its way slowly toward the structure. The defense units brought up the rear. For a moment, only Loba's back registered that he had heard. He turned, his expression inhuman. The master stared and did not speak.

Javek continued, "I must protest, sir. Bringing us all down to the planet in this manner is unacceptable. Why are we here? You must allow us to return to the ship immediately. If any harm comes to the *Galathea's* crew, the armed forces of Earth will respond. What...what are you?" She swallowed. "Your kind, whatever you are, whoever you are inhabiting our master and Stratton, you will not survive."

It was an empty threat, and Haggardy knew it. The officers looked fearful. Some were openly weeping. They were a long, long way from home, and the Global Government had little interest in the fates of prospecting crews. The employees took their chances and reaped their rewards or suffered the consequences of their deep space voyages.

Loba made no sound. He pulled a hand laser from his jacket. Javek backed away. The officers barely had time to scatter before he fired the weapon. Screaming, Javek fell. She crumpled to the ground and continued to cry out and writhe. Loba approached her. Was he going to finish her off? Haggardy was horrified and fascinated. But the master only inspected the injured officer. He spoke to a defense unit. "AX9, bring her."

The unit lifted the groaning Javek and put her over its shoulder. Loba's shot had scored a blackened line across the woman's right hip. Enough to incapacitate but not kill her. Haggardy guessed that Loba must want them alive.

His mind was working furiously. He had to think of an escape. He wondered if there was any residue of the master's original personality left behind. Could he appeal to the inner Loba? If he tried, maybe he would meet the same fate as Javek, who was being carried, sobbing, at the back of the line. In a few moments they would be at the structure.

Haggardy dropped back to the end of the line with Javek, acutely conscious of the weapons held by the units behind him. He could do nothing now, but perhaps, once they were inside, his options might open up.

He'd read Harrington's reports thoroughly. As they entered the structure, the plain gray walls and lightless rooms were no surprise. No alien life or artifacts. Nothing. He wondered how the mechanism for alien infection worked. Were they already being taken over?

"Press your hands to the walls," Loba said.

Cowering before the defense units, which had followed them, most of the officers obeyed immediately. The unit carrying Javek lifted her hands and pushed them against the wall. Haggardy hesitated, but Loba pointed the laser gun at his temple. He had no choice but to touch the cool metal/crystal amalgam with his open, bare palms.

As Loba turned to check on the other officers, a young cadet swung violently around and knocked the master to the floor. His weapon fell from his hand. Another officer immediately pounced on it and fired at a defense unit.

Another officer tackled Margret, but she brought a weapon up to his throat.

"Units, wound, don't kill," shouted Loba from his prone position. The cadet disappeared out of the door. Simultaneously, a unit fired on the officer who had picked up the master's weapon. The man shrieked as the laser beam severed his arm. Smoke and the scent of burnt flesh filled the enclosed space, and one or two officers gagged. Though the beam had partially cauterized the injured officer's wound, it steadily dripped blood. The man sank, gasping, to his knees. Loba plucked his weapon from the frozen fingers of the amputated limb.

Haggardy was loitering near the exit. He could see the cadet running back toward the shuttle, flinging dust from his heels. He would never make it. The defense units were too fast and accurate. Haggardy hesitated, then pointed at the young man. "Master," he said, "someone's getting away." His comment drew curses and exclamations of disbelief from the other officers.

Loba was out of the entrance in a trice. He instructed a defense unit to disable the cadet. The unit fired, hitting his shoulder. The man fell, but was quickly up and running again, though more slowly.

"AX15, retrieve that human," Loba said.

The named unit set off after the cadet, and Haggardy and the officers watched. AX15 was closing the distance to the racing man easily, despite being twice his bulk. But the cadet had a good lead. If he made it to the shuttle and locked himself in before being caught...if he knew how to fly the shuttle back to the ship...Haggardy began to sweat. The news of what he'd done might be passed on to the wrong people. His fingernails bit into his palms as he willed the unit to run faster.

"Come on, Arkady," murmured a voice. Other officers echoed the words. At the range and from their viewpoint, it was difficult to tell how far apart the unit and cadet were, but it looked like the man might make it. "Come on, hurry, please," whispered a voice nearby.

The unit stopped. Haggardy held his breath. Had it given up? Had it received a counter-command radioed from the *Galathea*? It was drawing its weapon. It fired, and the beam hit Cadet Arkady square in his back. The officers cried out.

AX15 stumped over to the fallen cadet and lifted him up. The officers watched silently as the unit returned with the young man, cradling him in his arms like an oversized doll. When the unit was in hearing range, it said, "Minor order deviation, Master Loba. I stunned Cadet Arkady in order to retrieve him."

17

Loba herded the officers into the next room and turned on a flashlight. He ordered the units to remain at the entrance. Two officers were told to drag the limp Arkady between them. The man was beginning to come around. Haggardy had no choice but to comply and go with the rest of them, but he'd made his switch of allegiance clear, and he hoped it would count for something. As Loba directed the officers through the next opening, and the next, Haggardy dropped back a little, slowing his pace until he was just in front of the master, who brought up the rear. Margret was leading the group.

"Sir," he said. Loba didn't acknowledge his words. "Is that what I should call you, sir?" When his question met no response, Haggardy decided to forge ahead, regardless of the dark glances the officers were throwing at him over their shoulders.

"As I understand it, you're taking us to be possessed by others of your kind. Am I correct? I wanted to tell you that for me, there's no need. I'm willing to come over to your side, as I showed you just now. I'm with you. And I can be useful. You'll need someone who understands how humans think and act. I can be your intermediary."

"Shut up, Haggardy," shouted a man. "Misborn coward."

The first mate made a mental note of the officer's name. He wouldn't forget it if they got out of this predicament unharmed.

"Sir," he continued, "I can give you information...data that doesn't exist in the ship's computer. Knowledge you can use. I..." Haggardy half-turned to look at Loba. The man's face was eerily underlit by the flashlight's glow. He wasn't even looking at him. He didn't seem to have heard a word Haggardy had said.

The first mate's hands began to tremble. Droplets of sweat appeared on his forehead, despite the freezer-like chill inside the structure. There was no point in appealing to whatever it was that possessed Loba. Haggardy's betrayal of the young cadet had been in vain. He silently cursed. After many successful years of appeasing those in authority, his methods were failing him.

Loba forced the officers deeper into the structure. Haggardy wondered if he was taking them to a special, central area that Harrington had failed to discover: a secret area, closed off from the rest. What might happen there, he did not want to dwell on. But now it was only Loba and Margret, and they had only two weapons. If Haggardy kept his wits about him, he might still survive.

The officers were becoming very cold. Javek was limping, and a man had her arm over his shoulders. The officer whose arm had been severed was staggering, dazed with pain. Haggardy diverted his mind from the others. He needed to concentrate. He was keeping a careful mental note of the turns they took and the number of rooms they passed through.

Haggardy had been born blind. He was a natural, and his blindness was just one of the many conditions modding would have prevented at conception, except that for his parents' generation, the process had been new and prohibitively expensive. So the young Haggardy had waited ten years for his parents to save up the money for the treatment to fix his sight problems. But the best cure available at the time couldn't undo all the effects of sightlessness during crucial stages of vision development. Haggardy had worn contacts all his life, something he never revealed to even his closest friends. At last, his childhood years of ridicule and shame might pay off. Though the memory of his blindness had lost its edge, he retained a measure of an ability to move around sightlessly.

They must have been a mile or more underground by then. Haggardy had figured out a pattern to the path they were taking. It was complex, comprised of fourteen steps, but the pattern had repeated three times, and he was sure he had it. If he could remember it, he might be able to make his way out in the dark and avoid the fate that Loba had in store for them.

"Stop," ordered the master. The officers must have worked something out in low whispers during their journey, for five or six of them turned and lunged at Loba. The ones at the front threw themselves on Margret. Haggardy stepped to one side, out of danger's way. Loba managed to kill three officers, but the flashlight fell to the floor, and from then onward, Haggardy saw nothing but dark, struggling shapes in the fight between Loba and Margret and the attacking officers. Everyone but the first mate joined in, adding new forms to the dark, writhing mass.

"Argh, my hand," shouted a voice. "I'm stuck to the floor." "I'm stuck too," called another. "I can't move." "Help," said a third. Officers were grunting in pain. "I can't let go of you." "Where's Arkady?" "I...argh...don't touch anyone. We're sticking to each other."

Shouts were turning to screams and shrieks. The beam from the flashlight shifted and rose. Loba had picked it up and turned it on the struggling officers.

"You...you monster. You freaks. What are you doing to us?" wailed a woman.

Loba played the flashlight around the room.

AN HOUR OR SO LATER, Loba and the officers emerged from the entrance to the structure, where the defense units awaited them. In single file, they marched to the shuttle. Haggardy was at the back of the line. After they had climbed up the ramp and into the passenger cabin, something that resembled the pilot, Grantwise, took the pilot's seat. The officers sat down and buckled their safety belts. The defense units surrounded them, but Loba didn't order them to train their weapons on the officers. Like the others, Haggardy sat looking forward, not speaking, his expression impassive.

18

Lee came jogging toward Jas and Lingiari as they left the area of the brig and headed for the bridge.

"Nice one, Navigator," said Lingiari as she approached.

"Stop," said Jas. "Wait a minute." She ran back to where the defense units were restraining the guards. She picked up the guards' weapons. "I think we'll be needing these." Returning to Lingiari and Lee, she held out one of the weapons for one of them to take while putting the other over her shoulder. They had no time to pay the armory a visit. Lee lifted her hands and eyebrows in alarm at the sight of the laser gun. Lingiari took it and peered at it. "I dunno how to—"

"Never mind," called Jas, running on. "Just point it like you mean it. I'll teach you later if I have to. I hope I don't. Come on."

"Shouldn't we bring the units with us?" asked Lee as she ran to catch up.

"Can't risk it," Jas answered. "If we meet a possessed

officer who ranks higher than me, the units will follow their orders. They'll turn on us."

The bridge was on the other side of the ship. They would have to cross the entire thin upper deck that lay above the *Galathea's* massive engines. Though it would have been possible to house the crew cabins, the hold, sample storage areas, auditorium, mission room, cafeteria, bridge, and so on all in one area, such as at the front or back of the ship, Polestar Corp preferred spreading out the occupied areas in order to provide healthy exercise for the crew. Their shipbuilding budget didn't stretch to a gym. Jas could easily have done without the exercise right that minute.

"I don't get what we're supposed to do when we get there," panted Lee.

"When that shuttle returns," replied Jas, "it's most likely going to be full of officers possessed by aliens. If we let them aboard the ship, we're sunk. The crew won't be able to tell them apart from unaffected officers like us, and most of them probably aren't even aware of what's happened. I don't know what the aliens have in mind, but whatever it is, we aren't going to be able to stop them once they're aboard. The crew will do whatever they say."

"So, what are we going to do?" asked Lee.

"If we get onto the bridge, we can put out a ship-wide alert. We can explain what's happening. If we try to talk to the crew one by one, no one will believe us, so we'll download the security camera vids of the defense units forcing the officers onto the shuttle, and show them on all channels. The crew will be warned. And we can stop the shuttle from docking."

"How are we going to do that?" Lingiari asked. "Close the shuttle bay doors?"

"Yes. And if they start to breach them, we can use the *Galathea's* plasma cannons."

"What?" Lee stopped dead. Lingiari also drew to a halt.

"You're saying we should fire on the shuttle?" asked Lingiari.

"But twenty or more officers are aboard," said Lee. "They might be infected by aliens, but they're human, Harrington. They're our friends and co-workers. We can't just kill them."

Jas faced the two across the corridor. "I understand how you feel, and I don't like it any more than you do, but what's the alternative? If they get aboard ship, we can't capture and confine them. They have units with them, units I can't command with Loba there. It would be impossible, and we'd all end up dead."

When neither Lee nor Lingiari answered, she continued running toward the bridge. The navigator and pilot soon began to catch up to her. She wondered if they would stick with her to the finish, no matter what. Could they fire on their shipmates and friends?

"Wait a minute," exclaimed Lingiari, "why don't we star-jump? The shuttle won't be able to reach the ship then."

"Of course," said Jas, slowing down. "If we leave now, when they get back, all they'll find is empty space. We can alert Polestar and explain to the crew what's happened in the safety of another star system. Great idea. You sure you can do it?"

"I'm a pilot, aren't I?"

It would take about half an hour to jog from the brig to the bridge, but there was plenty of time. Lingiari and Lee had broken her out of the brig around the time the shuttle had left. The round trip to the planet took hours, and Loba and the officers would be within the structure a long time too, according to Jas's observation of Loba's entrapment by

Margret. As soon as Lingiari was in the pilot's seat, he could start prepping the starjump engine. Lee could find the nearest safe star system and input the coordinates. They could jump in two hours or less.

Jas's conscience was eased. They wouldn't be forced to sacrifice the officers in order to save the rest of the crew. Maybe there would be a way of rescuing the possessed men and women at some point, too.

At last, the three officers drew to a halt at the bridge door. Lee gripped her sides and drew in lungfuls of air as Jas outlined her plan. She would enter first and fire off stun shots to quickly subdue whoever Loba had left in charge. Lingiari would back her up. Jas showed him how to fire his weapon and set it to stun. She wasn't sure what opposition they would encounter once they were inside, but their chances were good.

"Let's go," she said, slapping her palm to the security scanner. It flashed red and an alarm sounded. *Krat.* Loba had primed the security system. On-ship guards would already be on their way.

"Let me try," said Lee, but the door didn't open, and the alarm continued to sound. Lingiari's palm brought the same response. The noise was deafening. "We've triggered a shut down," shouted Lee.

"Krat, krat, krat," exclaimed Jas. She'd been focusing on what to do once they were on the bridge, not on how to get through the door. The escape for them and the remaining crew was on the other side, but it might as well have been light years away. Unless...? "Step back," Jas yelled. She aimed her weapon at the control panel.

"No," exclaimed Lee, as Jas blasted it apart. The door remained closed. "You've sealed it."

"I didn't know," said Jas. "Well, how about..." She lifted

the gun again and fired it square at the door. Paint blistered and oozed down, and the corridor filled with smoke. Lee and Lingiari stepped back. Soon, all three were coughing, and their eyes were watering. The metal beneath the paint turned black but was otherwise unaffected.

"Stop it," shouted Lee above the hum of the gun. "You're not gonna get through it that way, either."

"Why didn't you say something?" yelled Jas.

"I just did." She screamed and ducked as Jas swung her weapon toward her. The security officer fired off two shots, and cries of pain echoed from behind Lee. Two guards had appeared in the corridor, and Jas had shot them, leaving them unconscious.

"Watch out. More guards," said Lingiari. He was looking over Jas's shoulder. She turned and fired, blasting their weapons out of their hands.

"It's no good," said Lee. "We can't get in. We've got to leave."

Jas was forced to agree. "Where to?"

"This way," shouted the navigator, jumping over the unconscious guards.

"Where are we going?" asked Lingiari.

"The only place they'll never find us," replied Lee.

19

———

"Isn't this kinda dangerous?" asked Carl as he, Harrington, and Lee climbed down a narrow ladder that led down into the bowels of the *Galathea* and its engine maintenance tunnels.

"Yes, it is," Lee replied. "If the ship starjumps while we're down here, we're fried."

The copilot paused mid-step. Flux must have also heard the navigator's words, because he squirmed against Carl's chest.

Lee was above him on the ladder and didn't notice he'd stopped. She stepped on his head with her booted foot. "Hey, people coming through here. You can't just stop. Get a move on."

Carl looked down at the ladder. It stretched below them until it disappeared into the gloom. He looked up toward the closed service hatch they'd left behind some time ago. The tunnel they were descending through would have held four or five Carls crossways, but it didn't feel nearly large enough. "I don't think this is such a good idea."

"Keep going, Lingiari," called Harrington from her position on the rungs above Lee. "We've got to get out of sight before the shuttle returns. If Loba or one of the possessed officers finds us, they'll blast us off the wall."

"But—"

"Move it," commanded Harrington.

Carl's jaw tensed as he put a foot and a hand down onto the next rungs, and the next, and the next. The chief of security was losing all her former allure. He wondered why he'd ever been attracted to her.

"Of course it's dangerous," continued Lee. "Starship engines aren't designed to provide living conditions for humans. But this is the only place we have a chance of hiding out. The service tunnels are like a labyrinth. They could search for days and never find us, especially if we split up and keep moving."

"But what if they jump while we're in here?" Carl asked.

"My guess is that Loba wants to get all the crew down to the planet and infected before he goes anywhere," said Harrington. "That's going to take a couple of days."

"Your *guess*?" asked Carl.

"I think she's right," said Lee. "Let's get going. I don't like it anymore than you do. These rungs are disgusting, but we're better off saving our breath for getting down this ladder."

Carl continued grimly climbing down the ladder. His muscles were aching with the exertion, but he forced them to move. Wet with sweat, his palms were in danger of slipping on the rungs. A chain of lights that were embedded in the walls blinked on as they went. When they had climbed down about another fifty meters, Lee told him to look for tunnels branching off to the sides.

He'd been keeping his gaze fixed firmly on the wall fifteen

centimeters from his nose. Grimacing, he looked down to find the tunnels. The view swam before his eyes, and he gripped the rungs tighter. It was crazy. He was a pilot who was afraid of heights. He spotted the tunnels Lee had predicted, their dark entrances leading away from the main wall next to the ladder. "I can see them. We should've brought flashlights."

"No need," answered Lee. "The side tunnels are lined with the same motion-activated lights as this one, for the engineers. Just don't take the first one you get to. Don't be obvious. Pick one farther down, and we'll go from there."

Carl did as Lee suggested and swung off the ladder into the fifth tunnel he saw. Bending his head to avoid hitting the tunnel roof, he moved in to make room for Lee and Harrington. He realized why starship engineers were always short. Carl shifted the weapon he'd been carrying across his back to the front. Flux seemed to have fallen asleep, creating a soft bulge where the copilot's shirt met his pants. Lee maneuvered herself off of the ladder, and a moment later, Harrington joined the two of them.

The tunnel walls were made of metal gridwork, unadorned. A simple panel at the entrance bore the number 8.7.1.

"We made it," said Carl.

Harrington sat beside him and immediately cursed. "I'm an idiot," she added. "What am I thinking? I've got to go back."

"What? No," said Lee. "Loba and the others will be back soon. You can't risk it. If they find you, you won't stand a chance."

"But the defense units," said Harrington.

Lee groaned and leaned on the tunnel wall. "You're right. Why didn't I think of it? We're dead."

"What's wrong?" asked Carl, though he had a pretty good idea. He just wanted to be wrong.

"All Loba has to do is send the defense units down here to find us," said Harrington, destroying Carl's false hope. "Fifteen relentless, unstoppable androids. They'll keep looking until they locate us, and we can't destroy them. If we manage to hit them, they'll just retreat until they've healed enough to carry on."

"Would they really hurt you, Harrington?" asked Carl. "After you've commanded them for so long?"

"They're just machines," replied the security officer, "or as good as. They don't care about me. They'll follow Loba's orders. No one outranks him. And he doesn't even need to be with them. He can command them through the ship's comm system."

"No, wait," said Lee, "that's not true. Not if I can get to them first."

Harrington shook her head. "You can't override the command hierarchy protocol. If you try to tamper with it, they'll shut down. But then, that might not be so bad. No one'll be able to command them then."

"I won't need to override the hierarchy protocol if I can disable their comm links."

Harrington's eyes widened. "So they'll only respond to voice control?"

"Voice control only. Wait, no, forget it. They'll self-repair, right? Then we'll be back to square one."

"They will self-repair, but not immediately. We should have a window of a few hours at least. Let's do it." Harrington began to walk, stooping, to the abyss at the end of the tunnel and grabbed the ladder rungs. Lee followed her.

"Hold up," said Carl. "I'm coming too." He put a hand down his shirt and pulled out Flux, who blinked sleepily.

"What the...?" said Harrington, looking back at him. "I wondered what it was you had down there."

"I'll introduce you later," Carl said. He spoke to Flux. "Gotta leave you here for a while, little fella. Wait for me, but if I don't come back, well, you know what to do." He put the creature down. Flux folded his wings and turned his back on the copilot in reply.

Carl's muscles ached just at the thought of climbing all the way back up into the ship, but he swung the strap of his weapon out of the way over his shoulder. "Right behind you."

BY THE TIME he emerged through the service hatch and into the bright light of the corridor, some time later, his muscles were screaming at him. It took a lot more effort to climb up the ladder than down it, as it turned out.

Even Harrington seemed to be feeling the strain. Sweat had soaked through her uniform in dark patches, and she was looking pale and drawn. And Lee was in worse shape. The navigator looked as though she could barely stand.

"This way," said Harrington, setting off at a lope. Lee staggered after her. Carl pulled his weapon around and pointed it forward. News of their exploits had probably gotten out, and the crew would be on the lookout for them. He followed the two women. The engine access point was in an unfamiliar part of the ship, and Carl hoped the defense unit storage wasn't too far away. He also hoped they had a long time before Loba returned.

Their luck was holding. The crew members they

encountered backed away and ran at the sight of long-limbed Harrington bearing down on them, weapon at the ready. And it seemed that no one had thought of activating the defense units to capture them. Carl couldn't imagine Loba, even a possessed Loba, making such a mistake. He must have left behind only a few cadets on the bridge: terrified adolescents who were wondering what was going on.

When they reached the storage room, the defense units stood creepily in the half-light as they had when Carl had first commanded them. The scent of melted plastic from the unit the brig guard had shot tainted the air.

"All of them," exclaimed Harrington, turning on the light. "All fifteen are here. That means the shuttle must be back. We don't have much time before Loba figures out he can send them after us. All units, allow access to your CPUs. Lee, do your best."

A wide slot in the units' midriffs opened, but otherwise they didn't move. Lee was already at the nearest one, looking inside.

"How do you know how to do that?" Carl asked her, peering over her shoulder.

"I don't."

"What? Then how are you...?"

"We had android servants at home. I used to open them up and mess with them. Taught one of them to tap dance. I'm guessing defense unit CPUs are pretty much the same. I just need to find the receiving antenna and disable it. You keep watch with Harrington."

They'd left the door only slightly ajar. Harrington was peering out. Carl peeked over her shoulder, trying to get a view of the corridor.

Lee began humming last year's smash hit. It was the only noise for several minutes, except for Carl's heartbeat thumping in his ears. After what felt like a very long time, but was probably only a few moments, the navigator muttered a soft *Got it.*

"Give me your earring, Lingiari," said the navigator.

"Huh?" His hand went to the elongated platinum leaf he wore in his right ear.

"I need something sharp. Quick."

Carl pulled the jewelry free and passed it to Lee. He had a feeling it would be returned the worse for wear. Lee reached into the unit's midriff. A short screech of metal on metal made Carl wince. Lee moved to the next unit. A second later, there was another screech.

Then came the sound of approaching footsteps.

20

"Hurry up, Lee," said Jas quietly. Officers had appeared at the far end of the corridor. They had the same gait and fixed look that she'd seen with Loba and Margret. She closed the unit storage room door to a slim crack.

"Two down. Thirteen to go," said the navigator.

Jas's finger hovered over the trigger of her weapon as the officers approached. Were they looking for her, or the other two? Had they only come to retrieve the defense units? Loba would probably want to use them to force some more reluctant crew members onto the shuttle. Or were the officers on their way somewhere else?

"Eight to go," said Lee.

Jas's breathing quickened. The officers weren't going to pass by. They were looking at the door, looking directly at her, if they'd known it. At the last possible second, she switched her weapon to stun and slipped the barrel through the door crack. She fired. The leading officer collapsed. The rest reacted, but slowly, too slowly. She had time to stun another two before the rest fled. These aliens were still getting used to operating in human bodies.

Jas turned to see what was happening inside the room. Lee moved to another unit and put her hand in its chest, holding something silver in her fingers. Now that the infected officers knew they were in the defense unit storage room, it would only be moments until one of them comm'ed Loba. As soon as he got the message, he would—

"Last one," said Lee, stepping to the final unit. Simultaneously, it lifted an arm. Lee shrieked and backed up. She didn't move fast enough. The unit grabbed her throat and lifted her up. Her hand was in its chest. She choked and turned imploring eyes to Jas. The unit would snap the navigator's neck like a twig before she had time to swing her gun around, Jas realized.

A beam pulsed from Lingiari's weapon, hitting first one of the unit's arms then the other. Plastic and flesh burned, filling the room with smoke. Lee was turning purple. Her toes barely touched the floor.

"AX3, release Navigator Lee," commanded Jas.

Its fingers opened marginally. Lee had disabled the unit's CPU so that it no longer received Loba's commands, and it was trying to obey Jas, but Lingiari's close-range shot had disabled it. The slight movement of the unit's fingers was enough for Lee to pull herself free of its grip. She slipped out and down until her feet were flat on the floor. She rubbed her throat. "I did them all," she croaked.

A shot hit the door. It swung open. The officers had returned.

"All units, defend us from the adversaries in the corridor," shouted Jas, and stepped out of the way as the fifteen androids pushed past her, their weapons sliding into their hands. "Stun only," she added.

The fighting automatons did their job with practiced ease. The alien-infected officers barely got a shot in before the defense units laid them low. One at the back stopped trying to fight and turned to run. A stun beam caught him, and he fell. In less than a minute, the fight was over.

Jas counted the unconscious bodies. Twelve officers. At least twelve members of the ship's command had been possessed by an alien force. There had to be more. Loba would have kept some with him on the bridge.

But she couldn't worry about that now. They had only a short time before the master knew the defense units weren't responding to his commands through the comm system. "We need to get out of here with these units, before Loba turns up to counter-command me."

Lee was still rubbing her throat. She shook her head. "I've had it, Harrington. I can't go much further, and I certainly can't climb down into the engine again. You two go without me. I'll only slow you down." Her eyes were blood-shot from being choked, and exhaustion lined her face. Lingiari didn't say anything, but he looked as if he was at the end of his strength too.

Come to think of it, Jas realized, she was exhausted herself. Yet they had a hard run ahead of them before they were safe. The sight of the waiting units gave her the answer. Something she'd been tempted to do for fun, but had never dared to do for fear of losing all dignity. "Can you hold on to something? Grip on tight?" she asked Lee. "Do you have strength for that?"

"Hold on to what?" asked the navigator.

Jas motioned to a defense unit with her eyes.

"You mean...? No. No way."

"Come with me," said Jas, taking Lee by the hand and dragging her over to AX12. "Climb aboard." She grabbed the woman under the armpits—now wasn't the time for decorum—and told her to jump. As she hoisted the petite woman onto the back of the unit, Lingiari got the idea. He went over to AX6 and motioned Jas away as she approached. He clambered up by himself. Jas leaped onto AX10's back and commanded the units to return with them to the engine access point.

The fifteen units lumbered off, the corridor vibrating with their movement. "All units, anyone you see, except me, Lee or Lingiari, stun them." Jas's voice wobbled from the motion of AX10.

If they could get away fast, and if no one saw where they went, they had a chance, though she didn't know what their next step should be. They had to prevent Loba from taking the rest of the crew down to the planet somehow— "Wait, shuttle bay. All defense units to the shuttle bay."

With an abruptness that almost made her lose her grip, AX10 and the other units changed course.

"What are you doing, Harrington?" called Lee. "We can't go to the planet. We can't survive down there."

"We aren't going to the planet."

"What then?" asked the navigator, then her eyes widened. "Oh, I get it. Good idea."

"What?" Lingiari asked. "What are we going to do? Shouldn't we get back to the engine before Loba catches up with us?"

"We have to prevent him from getting the rest of the crew infected," said Jas.

"But how can we stop him?" asked Lingiari. "He only has to take them down to the surface, and he has his officer mates to help him now...Oh, no. Wait. No, no, no. We can't do that."

"We have to," replied Jas.

"There's gotta be another way."

"Sorry, Lingiari."

It was risky. It was crazily risky. But if they didn't act now, they would give Loba time to think it all out and get one step ahead of them. They had to do their worst while the ship was in disorder and the possessed officers were finding their feet.

The defense units could run faster than the fastest man. They brought the three humans to the shuttle bay within five minutes, encountering only a few crew members on the way. Most seemed to have fled the public areas.

Lingiari had gone very quiet during the journey, and Jas thought she saw tears in his eyes as they arrived at the shuttle bay. The bay was empty. They'd caught Loba out again. The copilot whimpered as Jas gave the order. "All defense units, fire on the shuttle, maximum power."

Blinding white light arched from the defense units' weapons. Their arms were more powerful than the weapons available to the crew. They were charged by the units' inner power core. The shuttle hull glowed scarlet, then white. The metal popped, fizzed, then began to melt as the units' beams breached the outer hull and penetrated the interior. Jas had to duck below AX10's back to shield herself from the heat of the destruction.

"Units, cease fire," she shouted and looked out. Through the smoke, the shuttle was little more than a white-hot ruin. Loba wouldn't be flying anyone anywhere in that ever again.

"Defense units, kill your passengers," came a voice from behind them.

Jas whipped around. A group of alien-infested officers had come up while they were destroying the shuttle. She recognized the fourth engineer, chief steward, and two or three uncertificated mates.

"Units, stun the approaching officers," she said, and held her breath. The units turned and aimed their weapons, and she exhaled. The officer who had commanded them was lower ranking than her. The fight was brief and decisive, and Jas commanded the units to return to their previous course.

As they passed through the group of fallen officers, Jas gasped. The last of the bunch was Haggardy. So the first mate had been infected too. He could have countermanded her and prevented himself and the others from being stunned. He could have stopped their destruction of the shuttle. Didn't the alien infecting him understand the ranking protocols? Or was it still getting used to Haggardy's body? Why hadn't it spoken?

21

———

The creature that looked like Loba reached out with its mind as it strode through the ship in the direction of the shuttle bay. It had arrived at the defense unit storage room too late. The human called Harrington and the ones who had disobeyed its order to go to the shuttle bay, Lingiari and Lee, they had taken the units. The creature could no longer communicate with them through the ship's system—a serious impediment to its plan. The defense equipment items were far superior in skill and strength than their human controllers. They had proven extremely useful, and the creature had anticipated using them for several more tasks in the suppression and replication of the remaining humans. But though the alien had made a grievous miscalculation in not accompanying the others to retrieve the units, the insurgent humans had made a worse one.

They had only made unconscious the others of its kind it had sent. They had not taken the opportunity to destroy them. Why this was so, the creature was not certain, but possibly the humans did not understand that they were only copies of the ones they had absorbed. Perhaps they imagined the dead humans lived on somewhere within the bodies they saw, and they had an attachment to them that prevented them from causing harm. If they were reluctant to damage the forms that the creature and the others had assumed, this would prove of great benefit.

The Loba creature was becoming aware of the minds of those it had left behind at the defense unit storage room. They were regaining consciousness. But it could detect nothing from the remaining ones that should be at the shuttle bay. It walked faster. It ran. The sensation of speed on the physical plane was dizzying and confused its senses. It reached out with its mind. Still nothing from the shuttle bay. Were those others unconscious? That could only mean one thing.

It had to protect the shuttle. The small ship was a precious item, and they needed it for transportation to the planet. Their numbers were not enough. They had to absorb and replicate more.

Signals from its olfactory organ. Knowledge from the copied Loba mind told the creature the signals indicated smoke. The smell of destruction. It was too late. It had failed again.

A second loss. Emotions flooded the creature. Anger. Fear. The humans who had destroyed the shuttle had guessed its intentions and subverted them. They knew what it wanted. It must locate the three humans responsible, and it must do so before they communicated their knowledge to the rest. It must end their lives as soon as possible. It would not wait to submit them to absorption and replication. They were too dangerous.

The odor of smoke grew stronger. In the corridor before the alien were the others it had sent to the shuttle bay, lying unconscious. It stepped through the bodies and made its way into the bay. The wreck of the shuttle sat at the center, its metal glowing, twisted, melted, scarred, scorched.

A beautiful artifact, destroyed beyond recognition. The Loba creature closed its eyes to shut out the sight of the ruin. The legs of the creature weakened. It found itself lying down. Their transportation to the planet was lost, but it was more than that. The shuttle was gone. Sorrow overwhelmed it. How could they do it? Humans were an evil species.

What should it do now? It had failed, failed, failed. It cast its mind wide, trying to contact and connect with the others of its kind, preparing itself for their censure. Separation was hard to bear.

22

———————

Jas surveyed her two human companions and fifteen defense units, deep within the labyrinthine maintenance tunnels of the *Galathea's* engine, taking stock of the situation. Lee and Lingiari were slumped on the metal gridwork, while the defense units sat on their haunches, too tall to stand.

Of the three officers, she was the only one trained in combat, but they had the units, and they were fully armed. They also apparently had some kind of weird alien creature that Lingiari had smuggled aboard. Trust him. The animal —what did he call it? Flux?—was hanging upside down from the tunnel roof, the claws of its feet clinging to the metalwork, its wings folded over its head. Beneath the transparent wings, its eyes and little sharp-toothed mouth were closed.

"I can't believe we did it," said Lee.

"Me neither," said Lingiari, holding a fist for Lee to bump. He next moved his fist to Jas, but she looked away. They didn't have time for this.

"You were awesome," said Lee to the copilot. "If you hadn't shot that unit, I'd be dead."

"Thanks. You weren't so bad yourself."

"How did you get to be such a good shot? I thought pilots only did basic combat training."

"Huh, it was pretty close range. Anyone could have done it, but I got a lot of practice when I was a kid growing up on the family farm. We had a rumpabug plague pretty bad. Used to take them out with a rifle while I was crop dusting, flying my dad's twin engine."

"What's a rumpabug?" asked Lee.

"You never heard of rumpabug? They were only the third worst alien infestation ever. We were overrun. You seriously never heard of them?"

"I was kind of sheltered as a child. All my parents cared about was—"

"How many officers went down to the planet with Loba?" Jas asked Lingiari.

"Err...nineteen or twenty."

"Is that counting Margret?"

"No," said the copilot.

That made at least twenty-two compromised crew members, including Loba and the geo-phys scientist, and about a hundred and eighty who couldn't be expected to do more than follow Loba's orders. While Jas, Lee, and Lingiari had two weapons, and the defense units with their inbuilt armory, the other side had the entire ship's arsenal. It was going to be a tough fight. Very tough. What was worse, they would be fighting their shipmates, their friends.

They had to act soon. It would be hard for Loba to find them now that they'd taken his best tools, but they couldn't last down there forever without water or food. They would be forced to steal supplies, and to do that they'd have to go out into the ship. The crew still didn't know exactly what was going on, and Loba would have them search the ship from top to bottom. Eventually, someone would figure out where they were hiding, and then Loba only had to post guards at each entrance hatch to the engine. Thirst and hunger would eventually force them out. Jas's eyes closed as she thought of a worse possibility.

"Geez, I'm bushed," said Lingiari. "I'm going to take a nap." He slid down the wall he was propped against and stretched out his lanky limbs.

"No, you can't," said Jas. "No time."

"Aw come on, Harrington. We've got to rest," said the copilot.

"Yes," said Lee. "If those units hadn't carried us down the ladders, I don't think I could have made it. We need to recuperate. I'm exhausted."

Jas tutted internally. This was why she preferred working with defense units. They never complained, and they never questioned orders. "Look," she said, an edge to her voice, "Loba probably has the entire crew looking for us right now. How long do you think it's going to take for them to realize where we must be? And what do you think he'll do when he knows we're here?"

A silence. Lee blanched. "Start the engines and starjump?"

"He might," replied Jas. "I'm not sure that he would, but it's a possibility. I think he's going to want to get the rest of the crew infected, which means sticking around this planet. But he could starjump and come right back. He has the math for at least the next two jumps in the computer, right?"

Lee nodded glumly.

"As long as the infected crew are a minority, he knows he's at risk of us convincing the rest about what's happened," continued Jas. "He knows we could gather the crew for a mutiny. The safest thing for him to do is to get everyone possessed as quickly as he can."

"But he can't now that we've destroyed the shuttle," said Lee.

"He can. The shuttle wasn't the only way of getting down to the planet."

"Of course," Lee said. "He could fly the ship down."

"Woah," said Lingiari. "Fly the *Galathea* through a planetary atmosphere? Deal with planetary gravity? Starships aren't made for it. RaptorX engines are only intended for orbit adjustment and interplanetary travel. Grantwise'll never do it."

"He'll try, that's my best guess," continued Jas. "But if he does that, we won't be in immediate danger. He'll just be burning rocket fuel, not starting the starjump engine. And the RaptorX engines are way astern of us. Loba'll have to force us out another way. He might turn off the lights."

"Can the defense units navigate in the dark?" asked Lee.

"Yes, it won't matter to them, but we're handicapped without light, and we need supplies. We can't stay here indefinitely. We have to do something, and it has to be soon, before Loba knows where we are."

"Okay," said Lingiari, sitting up. "What do we do?"

Jas bit her lip and looked from the navigator to the copilot. "We can't risk trying to talk to the crew to convince them about what's going on. Loba will have spun them a story to explain what's happened and pin the blame on us, and they're more likely to believe the master than someone who's been locked up in the brig, or either of you. Loba and the others don't look any different, after all. As soon as we go near any of the crew they're going to jump on us and ask questions later, or not at all. There's no other option. We have to take control of the ship."

"By ourselves?" Lee asked. "How the hell are we going to do that?"

That was the hard part. "To be honest, I don't know," replied Jas. "Look, I can't figure this out by myself. I need you two to help me. Lee, you knew about this place. Do you know the rest of the ship's layout as well?"

"I think so. Most of it."

"Is there an interface with the ship's system down here? Can you deactivate the bridge door from here, for instance?"

"There have to be system access points around here for the engineers, but they won't be any help. Loba ordered a security update, remember? We're all locked out of the system now."

"Krat, you're right. Well, we've just got to get onto the bridge and stop Loba from taking the ship down to the planet. The sooner the better. If he manages to get more of the crew infected, it's over. And we have to take out the rest of the officers."

"Wait a minute," said Lee. "What do you mean by 'take out'? You don't mean we're going to kill them?" She and Lingiari exchanged a look.

"I'm sorry, but if it comes to that, yes, we'll have to kill them." Not this again. Jas raised her voice over Lee and Lingiari's protests. "I made a mistake back there when we were retrieving the units. Stunning only lasts five minutes, and there are more than twenty of them. If we don't take them out permanently we'll never defeat them."

"Gee, Harrington," said Lingiari, shaking his head, "I don't know about that. I don't think I could—"

"They're possessed by aliens, and if we don't do something they're going to get the rest of the crew infected, and then they could return the ship to Earth so the aliens can overrun the whole planet, or spread across the entire galaxy."

Lee was frowning, and Lingiari still looked doubtful. "Couldn't we round them up? Put them in the brig?" suggested Lee. "Maybe Dr. Sparks has some idea how to—"

"Sparks is a useless gasbag," said Jas. "Do you think Loba's going to just stun us?" She closed her eyes and pressed her lips together. She tried taking a deep breath, but it was no good. She couldn't believe Lee and Lingiari were being so obtuse. Couldn't they see the danger everyone on the *Galathea* was in?

"We don't have time for this," she exclaimed before continuing, between her teeth, "We just don't have time. We need to mount a coordinated attack on Loba and the infected officers, now. Both of you have to lead a team of units. We have to move fast. Lee, where are all the exits from the service tunnels?"

The navigator stuttered a reply, adding, "There's no call for losing your temper, Harrington."

Maybe she was a little testy, but she couldn't help that. She couldn't afford to take people's feelings into account when it came to saving the crew. Why couldn't Lee or Lingiari see that?

23

Sayen's heart felt like it was going to jump right out of her chest. She gripped the ladder rungs tightly as she fought to control her rising fear. At least she didn't have to carry a gun. At least she wouldn't be forced to kill one of her shipmates—maybe someone she'd eaten dinner with, or sat next to on the bridge, or laughed at holos with on entertainment nights. But the six defense units clinging to the ladder above her, the ones she was supposed to command...Harrington had told her to instruct them to use lethal force if necessary. She wouldn't be killing anyone, but the units she was commanding might. She wasn't sure if that was different.

When she'd helped to break the security officer out of the brig, and when they'd taken the units, they had been acting fast, thinking only a step ahead. Standing on the ladder, waiting for the moment she was supposed to follow the units out into the ship, she had time to think about what might happen, and none of the possible scenarios gave her comfort.

Someone might end up dead. Maybe her. Or Loba might

force her to be infected by an alien. She shuddered so hard she nearly lost her grip. Her sweaty palms made holding on difficult. She dared not look down to the gloomy depths of the tunnel below her.

What wouldn't she give to be in her neat, clean cabin right then. She was filthy, and her skin crawled at the thought of all the germs that must be on her skin.

It couldn't be much longer until the time they'd agreed they would exit the tunnels. Were they doing the right thing? She wished she'd had time to think it through, to talk it out with both of the others, but the security officer had been insistent that this was the only way. Harrington was scary when she was angry, and Sayen didn't have the guts to stand up to her. Neither did Lingiari.

That was the worst of it. What if there was a better way? What if there was a way they could avoid killing the infected officers, but she just hadn't had time to think of it? If only she could talk to Lingiari. They could team up and persuade Harrington to call the attack off, to reconsider. But she had removed her comm hours—seemingly days—ago, and the copilot had done the same.

Her muscles were so sore, and she was thirsty and hungry. She wondered—

The lights went out. Sayen froze. The crew must have searched the ship. Loba must have guessed where they were. A clang came from above, and a square of light appeared in the darkness. This was it. The defense units had been told that if the lights went out, they were to begin the attack immediately. A defense unit above passed through the hatch it had opened, momentarily plunging them back into darkness.

Sayen had no choice but to follow.

She emerged from the hatch. The units were moving

fast, and she struggled to keep up as they pounded away from her. The sound of firing came from in front. Loba must have sent guards to intercept them.

How were Harrington and Lingiari faring? Had they even made it out?

The shooting stopped. Sayen raced to catch up to the units. She had to be near them so they could hear her orders. The heels of the last unit were disappearing around a corner. As Sayen turned the same corners she halted abruptly. Two shipmates lay on their backs in the corridor. One was missing the top of her head. The other had a gaping hole in his chest. She recognized them both. They were infected officers, not crew, but still she felt like she was going to vomit.

The pounding of the defense units' feet broke her distraction. They were getting away. She began to sprint. The sounds of more firing came from ahead.

Harrington had given her the easiest of the three attack routes, in view of the fact that she had no weapon to defend herself with. The security officer had speculated that Loba and his officers would either congregate on the bridge, the mission room, or the auditorium, where he could address the crew. They were to attack all three.

She'd been allocated the task of assaulting the mission room, where Loba could access all the files on planets on their schedule and auxiliary files about Earth. Not only was the mission room the attack site closest to the engine access hatch, it was also the smallest of the three rooms and likely to contain the fewest hostile crew members.

Aside from the two infected officers the defense units had killed, the corridors were empty. Either Loba had gathered the crew in the auditorium, or they'd been ordered to stay in their cabins. Sayen was grateful for it.

She was running as fast as she could, but hadn't had enough time to rest and recover. She was much too slow, and the defense units had drawn far away from her. Out of sight. She should have asked one of them to carry her, but she couldn't help that now. She rounded another corner. There it was: the mission room. But there was no sight nor sound of the units. The door was open, but from the angle of her approach, she couldn't see inside. Was it possible the units had gone the wrong way? No, that was ridiculous. Had Loba left the room unguarded? Had she lucked out and there was no one inside?

She drew to a stop just outside, where she had a slim view of the interior. The view told her nothing. Only the walls were visible to her. It was no good. She was going to have to put her head around the door.

She was gasping loudly in the silence. If anyone was in there, they were sure to hear her, to know someone was there. They must have heard her running up, too.

Holding her breath, Sayen shot her head forward. At an equal speed, she drew it back, just in time. A laser bolt came through the door exactly where her head had been and burned the wall on the opposite side of the corridor. The sound of more firing burst from the room, accompanied by screams and cries. Sayen stood with her back to the wall, splayed against it. More cries, shots, thumps of bodies hitting the floor. She thought she recognized some of the voices. One was the third mate, she was sure of it.

Silence. An awful stink came from the room, which Sayen suspected was the smell of burned human flesh. She was sickened. Footsteps. Someone was walking to the door. She should run. She had to run, or they would kill her. But her legs wouldn't move. She mentally screamed at her limbs, but it was as if they belonged to another body. There was nothing she could do. She was going to die.

Sayen closed her eyes as the footsteps reached the door. She didn't want to see which of her former colleagues was going to kill her.

But the fatal shot didn't come.

"Navigator Lee, the room is secure."

Sayen opened her eyes. A defense unit was standing before her, its large form blocking out the overhead lights. She peeled herself from the wall and peeked into the room.

Four officers lay dead. One defense unit was down, its silicon/organic brain exposed in its helmet. Four units had their weapons trained on the third mate, who was on his knees with his hands in the air.

"Shoot her, kill her," exclaimed the man. When the units didn't respond, he said, "Defense units, kill Navigator Lee."

"We are unable to comply," said a unit. "Navigator and third mate rank equally. We must follow Regulation 723g of Defense Unit Lethal Behavior Protocols: *When an officer threatens the life of an officer of equal rank, the officer whose life is threatened assumes supersedence.* When you observed Navigator Lee at the door and tried to shoot her, her command immediately superseded your own. Navigator Lee's order was to secure this room with the use of lethal force if necessary."

The four units that were pointing their weapons at the third mate raised them to fire.

"Units, no. Don't shoot," said Sayen. "Don't shoot him."

The third mate's gaze rested on the navigator. Something was wrong about the way he looked at her. There was nothing behind his eyes. Nothing at all. The hairs along her spine rose.

The sound of running footsteps came from the corridor.

Sayen tensed. Harrington? But why would she come here? They were supposed to rendezvous at Margret's cabin. Could it be Lingiari?

It was neither. Master Akabe Loba appeared in the doorway, panting. He pointed a trembling finger at Sayen. "Units, kill that officer."

24

Carl wondered how he'd gotten into his current position, staring into the massive soles of a defense unit on the ladder above him. Harrington's order to kill the infested humans if necessary didn't seem right. And who was she to boss them around? His opinion of the security officer had changed. He'd always found her quick temper kind of exciting, but it wasn't so attractive when it was directed at him.

He would have been better off with Margret. Poor Margret. What if she attacked him? He didn't think he could kill her. Or any of the others for that matter. Even Loba, though—

Flux wriggled against his chest, adjusting his position in Carl's shirt. The animal had insisted that he came along too. His fur tickled, but apart from that the copilot was glad to have him. He'd adopted the little fella—or rather he'd chosen to come live with Carl, as he put it—when Carl was a kid. Flux had flown into his open cockpit while he was out dusting crops one day, giving him quite a fright. The animal had never said where he was from, only that he was taking a long holiday on Earth while 'things cooled down' on his home planet. When he arrived in Carl's cockpit his accent had been British, so he must have spent some time with the Poms, but over the years Flux had acquired Carl's Strine.

"You sure about this, mate?" Carl asked the lump in his shirt.

"Yeah, you're not leaving me behind this time, you dumb…" Flux swore. He could swear like a space marine and wasn't slow to share his opinion. Luckily, he was also prone to long sulks, when he refused to speak. Something that came in handy if Carl had a new girlfriend around.

The lights went out, which meant Loba knew where they were. From above came the sound of a hatch clanging open. The defense units began to make their way out.

Carl swiftly climbed the ladder on the tail of the units, hoping Harrington had reached her exit before Loba cut the lights. The engine maintenance hatch she was taking was right on the other side of the ship, near the bridge. He didn't know what her plan was to get onto the deck, considering they'd failed at that before. His target was the auditorium, where Loba or another officer might have gathered the crew.

In a few moments, Carl was through the hatch, out into the corridor, and hard on the heels of the units. The units had shot two crew members. *Krat.* They weren't even infected officers. Loba had already drafted some of the crew into his schemes. Carl's fingers tightened on his weapon as he sprinted after the units. He saw no one as he ran. He hoped the rest of the crew would act smart and stay the hell out of the way.

Flux was climbing out of his shirt, and Carl winced as the creature's claws tugged his chest hair.

"What are you doing?" he asked.

"I'm gonna help, aren't I?" replied Flux. He scrambled

onto Carl's shoulder and leaped off, taking to the air. The animal could fly faster than Carl or even the units could run, and he soon disappeared from view.

Carl sprinted to keep up with the pounding pace of the units, adrenaline cutting through his exhaustion. The auditorium was near. He turned a corner. The units had disappeared from view. They were in the auditorium. Carl heard screams and shouts and the sound of many people moving around. Harrington had guessed right. The crew was in there. Flux came flying out of the room and straight at Carl.

"Run," he shouted as he passed overhead. "You got first prize. Loba's in there."

Carl didn't need telling twice. He skidded to a halt and reversed direction before belting away. Harrington had been crystal clear: if they encountered Loba, they had to get out of there fast. Loba would turn the defense units from their best allies to their worst enemies. The voice of the master came from behind, shouting, "Units, kill Lingiari." Loba must have stepped out of the auditorium in time to catch a glimpse of Carl running away.

But the copilot was gone, racing down the corridor. He didn't stand a chance against seven defense units. He could never outrun them, and as soon as they got a visual on him, he'd be dead. He had to find somewhere to hide.

Where? The doors to either side of the corridor were closed and he couldn't waste even a split second trying to open any of them. He wanted to call out to Flux, to see if the animal had a suggestion, but he had no breath to spare, and his little mate was out of sight. Probably just as well. It looked like it was game over for Carl. The adrenaline that had lent him speed couldn't push his exhausted muscles much farther.

A pale brown shape fluttered briefly into view from a

side corridor before disappearing again, leaving the words, "This way, mate," hanging in the air. *You beaut.* Carl squeezed one last effort from his painful legs and put on an extra spurt, slipping down the corridor just as he heard the units enter the one he'd left.

To his right was an open door and a beckoning hand. It shot out and grabbed his arm, and Carl stumbled into the room. The door clicked closed as pounding feet approached in the main corridor. The copilot had collapsed on the floor. A man helped him sit up. He held his knees and sat gasping, unable to speak for several moments. Finally, he managed, "Thanks...?"

"Alef, geo-phys," said the waiting man. He held out his hand and pulled Carl to his feet. "I've been watching out for you guys, hoping I could help. I was going into the main corridor to bring you here when your little friend happened to fly by. He told me to stay where I was and that he'd get you."

Carl clasped Alef's hand once more. "Lucky you did. Much too dangerous for you out there. Thanks, you old... " He swore.

Alef's eyebrows rose.

"Sorry, I was talking to Flux." The animal was hanging from the ceiling and grooming his belly fur. Carl added, "You said you're geo-phys, like Margret?"

"That's right. I'd been hoping someone would..."

Carl held up a finger to silence him. The sound of the units' footsteps had faded, which meant Carl might have a chance at a bigger prize. He went to the door and opened it the slimmest crack. He put his eye to the opening. It was not long before he saw Loba stride past in the main corridor following in the path of the defense units, probably trying to catch up to them so that he could control them with voice commands. Carl mouthed the master's name to Alef, opened the door wide and motioned for him to come closer.

The geo-phys scientist nodded his understanding. As one, the men ran out and after the master. They tackled him from behind. Alef grabbed him round his thighs, sending him toppling to the floor. Carl landed with his knees on the man's back, forcing the air from his lungs. Alef reached for the weapon the master had strapped to his hips, pulled it out and flung it down the corridor.

Carl wasn't a trained fighter, but he'd seen enough hand-to-hand combat in video games to last him a lifetime. He got Loba in a chokehold to stop him from speaking. If he called back the defense units, it would be all over for them. Together, they dragged the struggling man into Alef's room.

When Alef let go of Loba's legs to close the door, the master took his chance and kicked him in the head, sending him crashing into the wall. With a great wrench, Loba broke free. He ran to the door and bellowed, "Defense units, return to—" His words were cut short as Carl rammed into him, sending him through the door and into the corridor wall. The master's head made contact face first with a crack, and blood streamed from his mouth and nose as he staggered to his feet.

Loba turned and sucked in a breath to shout again, but Carl punched him in the jaw. He reeled back.

A shout came from the end of the corridor. The second mate had followed Loba. He was pointing a gun at Carl, who immediately grabbed Loba and shielded himself with the master's body.

The second mate advanced, and Carl backed up, dragging the struggling Loba with him, one hand clamped like a vice over his mouth. If only he had a weapon...but of course, he did have one. All this time, he'd been carrying the weapon Harrington had taken from the guard at the brig. He'd strapped it across his back. But if he wanted to grab it, he would have to loosen his grip on the master.

The two parties moved slowly down the corridor, the second mate advancing on the pilot and master. The officer passed Alef's room, and the geo-phys scientist crept out and picked up the gun he'd taken from Loba. He lifted and aimed it at the second mate. "Drop it."

Spinning to face the threat behind him, the second mate fired. At almost the same moment, Alef returned fire. Both Alef and the second mate fell, and the moment's distraction this caused Carl was all it took for Loba to free himself. He didn't waste time by fighting the copilot, but took off down the corridor, shouting for the defense units.

Carl cursed and ran to Alef. The second mate had winged him, but he was still alive. The officer who had shot him hadn't fared so well.

"I'm all right. Go after Loba," said Alef.

There was nothing Carl could do but follow the master and try to capture or kill him. He just hoped the defense units' great speed had taken them far beyond the reach of his voice. If no one had ordered them to do anything different, they would still be searching for Carl. He pulled forward the weapon that hung across his back and set off.

He didn't have to go far to catch up to Loba. Only a couple of corridors away was the mission room. Loba was standing at the entrance. He was pointing inside. As the words, "Units, kill that officer," left his lips, Carl shot him.

25

The lights went out. *Krat.* "Defense units, go, go, go," shouted Jas, even as the unit at the top of the ladder opened the hatch and vaulted into the corridor. Above her, the rest of the units poured through the hatch in turn. She raced up the ladder. Laser fire from above told her that guards had been posted.

Jas leaped out and barreled down the corridor. It was a ten-minute walk to the bridge. The units would be there in two. A door opened to her right. The medical center. Sparks looked out.

"Get inside and barricade yourself in," called Jas over her shoulder as she flew past. She wondered what the doctor thought of her mental state now. The units were getting away. She sprinted, her weapon flying behind her on its strap.

Her only hope was that the high-power lasers of the defense units would burn through the reinforced bridge door. If they got through and onto the deck, she stood a good chance of gaining control of the ship. If they couldn't get access to the flight controls, it wouldn't matter if they took out Loba and every other infected officer.

The sound of weapon fire came from up ahead. The units must have reached their destination or encountered resistance on the way. Jas tried to ignore the guilt that arose at the thought that the units might be killing shipmates. None of this was the crew's fault. But if she was going to save the rest of them, it had to be done.

Something hard and heavy struck the back of her head. The floor of the corridor rose up toward her face, and the next thing she knew, she was on her front, nose pressed to tile. Someone was holding her wrists. She forced her arms apart and tried to get up. The strap of her weapon caught on her neck as someone removed it.

"She's coming round," said a voice.

Jas struggled to turn onto her back, but a knee was thrust into the space between her shoulder blades, and an adult's full weight pressed down on her. She could barely breathe.

"Let me go," she gasped.

Strong hands grabbed her wrists once more.

"Keep still, or I'll melt your brains," said another voice. It was the man kneeling on her back. She could see the feet and lower legs of other crew members standing around. From down the corridor came the sound of more firing. The defense units were in a pitched battle, and she wasn't there to command them. Without her order to withdraw, they would fight to gain access to the bridge until they were put out of action, maybe permanently.

"He was right, wasn't he?" said a voice to her right. "He said she might come down this way. Smart guy, that Loba."

"Let me up, you idiots," croaked Jas. "It isn't the master

who told you to capture me. He's been taken over by an alien. Most of the senior officers are possessed."

"BF. You're the one who's been possessed," said the man holding her down. "And he didn't tell us to capture you. He said to shoot you on sight. Only some of us were a bit queasy about that, so it's thanks to our kind hearts you're still alive. But you keep struggling and that can soon change."

"Krat." For a moment, Jas relaxed her muscles. The man's knee ground harder. If he didn't get off her soon she would pass out. "Okay," she gasped. "I won't struggle."

"What's that she's saying?" asked her captor.

"I dunno." Someone's head lowered near hers.

The world was turning black. "I give up," whispered Jas.

"Says she gives up," repeated a voice.

"That's more like it," said the man. Mercifully, the pressure on Jas's chest lifted.

"Is it okay if I get up?" she asked when she could speak again. Anger at her captors had begun to boil inside her. Just a short distance away, her defense units were engaged in battle, and they didn't have her guidance.

"All right. Just move slowly."

Jas turned over, and soon she was sitting with her legs drawn up, facing the crew who had ambushed her. There were four of them. Two male, two female. All had weapons. One was also holding hers. They were looking pleased with themselves, especially the one who'd been kneeling on her back. He had a particularly annoying grin on his face. He was the biggest and strongest of the four. Slowly, she got to her feet.

"You're not in the brig yet," the man said. "You better watch your moves. If you try anything, I might decide to follow Loba's order to the letter."

"I don't know what the master's told you," said Jas, "but, really, it isn't me who's been taken over by something, it's him."

"Well you would say that, wouldn't you?" said the man.

"I know I can't prove it to you, but...do you know he took the senior officers down to the planet? Have you ever heard of that happening before? I don't know how long you've been working aboard prospecting ships, but that literally never happens. If something were to go wrong and all the officers were planetside, can you imagine the danger we might all be in? It's totally against regulations."

"We destroyed the shuttle to stop Loba from taking the rest of you down and getting you infected by aliens too. We were trying to save you." An edge had crept in Jas's voice. If these fools didn't let her go soon, her only chance to get onto the bridge would be gone.

"Ha, that's where you're wrong," said the man. "It was Loba who destroyed the shuttle, to stop *you* from taking us down there."

"Wait a minute, Karrev," said the other man. "He only told us that. It could have been them, like she says. He seemed pretty mad about it. How do we know who did it? No one saw. And I heard a rumor that the officers were away during the quiet shift."

"No, he's the master," countered Karrev. "How would he get infected by an alien? He'd never be so stupid as to put himself in danger. She's the one whose job it is to go down there. She's the one at risk from aliens."

Jas's fury boiled over. "Don't be so stupid. Of course Loba could've put himself in danger. The man's a myth addict. Everyone knows it. He's unstable, unpredictable, and incompetent. He did go down. He was persuaded to, and now he's possessed. You have to let me go so I can save your sorry asses."

The man's brow furrowed "Maybe you're right and you haven't been infected by an alien. Maybe you just want command of the ship, and all this talk about the master being possessed is a trick to get us to commit mutiny." He pointed the gun between her eyes. "The brig, now, or say goodbye. You choose."

Jas's shoulders sagged, and she took a step toward the man. Interpreting her movement as acquiescence, his eyes flicked triumphantly to his friends. At that instant, Jas lunged forward and under his weapon, forcing him against the wall. The laser gun fired and scorched a line across the ceiling. The man's companions stepped back in alarm. Jas grabbed his arm and wrist and twisted them so his weapon was pointing at his face. Her forearm was across his throat, and she held him immobile, his gun centimeters from his nose.

The man gave a cry and thrashed his legs, kicking Jas's shins. She didn't blink. With her full weight and strength on him, he was helpless. After a few moment's struggle, while his shipmates stood frozen in indecision, the man released his weapon. It slipped from his fingers, and Jas grabbed it as it fell. She stepped back and fixed the barrel on the man. "Go," she shouted to the crew. "Drop your guns, and go. That way. Run, or I'll blow his kratting head off."

With only a second's hesitation, the remaining man and both women took off in the direction Jas had indicated.

"Don't...don't," said the man, his gaze on the barrel's end in his face.

"Of course I'm not going to hurt you. If you'd just listened to me, it wouldn't have come to this." The sounds of the battle for the bridge had ended several moments before. Jas had to find out what had happened. She scooped up her weapon from the floor, set the man's gun to stun, shot him, and was on her way before his body hit the floor.

26

A familiar smell assaulted Jas's nostrils and alerted her to the outcome of the battle for the bridge before she reached her destination. Laser fire on defense units fried their organic, plastic, silicon, and metal parts, creating a unique odor: part refuse dump fire, part barbecue. As always, it made Jas nauseous.

Swallowing the increased saliva in her mouth, she stopped. Judging by the reek drifting down the corridor, and the fact that none of the units had come to find her and give a combat report, she concluded that they'd failed to gain access to the bridge. Loba must have concentrated his defenses there, protecting the *Galathea's* flight controls and Grantwise. If that was the case, her guess that he would try to land the *Galathea* on K. 67092d was probably correct. The aliens could then take over the rest of the crew, but if Lingiari was right and landing a starship on a planet was nearly impossible, they were going to crash and everyone, infected and uninfected, would die.

She crept forward, a gun in each hand. All was silent. At each corner, she stopped and peered cautiously around. A short distance from her goal, she spotted an infected officer. She was armed.

Jas withdrew quietly. She could shoot and kill or stun the officer easily, but what would be the point? If the defense units couldn't get onto the bridge, she didn't stand a chance by herself. It was no good. Time to retreat and regroup. Turning, she ran softly away and figured out the fastest route to the planned rendezvous point, hoping that, even though she had failed, Lee and Lingiari might have succeeded, hoping they were still alive.

What she found at Margret's cabin surpassed her expectations. On the floor was a bound and gagged Loba. The copilot was sitting on him.

"We ordered our defense units to return to the maintenance tunnels," said Lee, "in case he got free."

"Good thinking," said Jas. She squatted down next to the prone Loba. His eyes were bloodshot. He looked furious, but the gag kept his thoughts silent. With him as a hostage, maybe their prospects weren't so bleak after all. "What about the crew?"

"They scattered like gene dealers in a raid," said Lingiari.

The copilot and navigator briefly told her what had happened. "I nearly died," said Lee. "I had everything under control, then Loba turned up. He told the defense units to kill me. I thought I'd had it, but they didn't obey. I don't know why. Then Lingiari shot him."

The master didn't seem injured. "You stunned him?" Jas asked the copilot.

"Yeah, I know what you said," replied Lingiari, "about how stunning them wasn't enough, but..." He shrugged.

"It's okay," said Jas. "I get it. And it might have worked in our favor this time."

"How come the units didn't follow his order to shoot me?" asked Lee.

"Did he preface his command?" Jas asked in return. "Remember what I said? If you don't address them first, they won't do as you say. I can't imagine the kind of trouble we'd be in if they did whatever someone around them said."

"Yeah," said the copilot, "like, bugger me sideways."

The two women looked at him.

"It's just a joke."

"This isn't the time for joking, Lingiari," said Jas.

"I'm pretty sure he did address them first," said Lee, "but he said, *kill that officer*. They probably didn't know who he meant. The third mate was there, too. So they didn't fire. Lucky me. But what are we going to do with him? Take him into the engine with us? I don't know how we'll get him down a ladder tied up like this."

Loba gave a great wrench and tried to squirm out from under the copilot. Lingiari grabbed the man's white curls and pushed his face into the floor. "Better cut that out, mate."

"We can't take him down into the engine service tunnels," said Jas. "We can't let him anywhere near the defense units, and we don't have time for a long-term strategy. I couldn't get onto the bridge, but we have to, and soon. We have to get Grantwise away from those controls."

"Is there an autopilot?" asked Lee. "Could he activate it and lock it even if we get onto the bridge?"

"Yeah, there's an autopilot, but you can't lock it in to land on a planet. That's the last thing you'd want to do in an emergency," Lingiari replied. "That's not the problem. Look, to pass pilot training you've gotta land the simulator ship as if you were landing on Earth, just once, using the RaptorX engines. Took me twelve tries, and I was one of the better ones. That planet below us isn't Earth, and while Grantwise might stand a chance of landing on it without crashing on a good day, I can't speak for that thing inhabiting him."

"That decides it," said Jas, standing up. "Come on. Bring Loba. We're going to the bridge."

"What's the plan?" asked Lee as they pulled the master to his feet.

Lingiari grabbed one of Loba's arms and pointed the muzzle of his weapon at his head. Jas held her weapon to the other side as she also grabbed an arm. "Simple," said the security officer. "If they don't let us onto the bridge, we kill him." Loba struggled as they half-pushed, half-dragged him out of the cabin.

"But what if they don't care?" asked Lee.

"You think they won't care if we kill him?" asked Jas. "But he's their..." Her words dried as she realized what the navigator meant.

"Loba's our master, doesn't mean he's theirs," said Lee. "We don't know what status the creature inside him has. He might be a nothing. Or they might not pay individuals any mind. The aliens could be a community species, and he's only one unimportant individual."

"Krat," said Jas. "For someone who's terrified of aliens, you sure know a lot about them."

"That's *because* I'm terrified of them. Know your enemy."

Lee had made a good point. Jas was assuming the aliens would act like humans. Mistake number one in the starship security officer manual. How could she have been so dumb? Maybe it was because she was used to aliens that looked like aliens. "Do you have a better plan?"

"No, I was just pointing out the problem," said the navigator.

"Gee, thanks."

Loba was struggling like a wildcat as they dragged him along. He tripped and fell, landing on his knees. Jas found grappling him to his feet while holding onto her weapon to be a struggle. Lingiari was doing his best to help, but he was also holding a weapon in one of his hands. Before she knew it, the master had slipped from their grasp and managed a few steps. It was several moments before Jas and the copilot could get him under control again. The thing inhabiting Loba certainly seemed to fear what would happen when they got to the bridge. Maybe Lee was right and the rest of them would let her fry his head. If that happened, she, Lee, and Lingiari were toast too.

Jas took comfort in the cool, smooth feel of the weapon in her hand. If the worst came to the worst, she would get as many of them as she could before she went down.

They were nearly at the bridge. "Hey," she shouted. "Hey, whatever you are, we've got Loba, our master, so we've got whichever one of you that's inside him. And we'll kill him if you fire."

"Maybe," Lee piped up, "maybe I should stay back? In case...you know?" The navigator suddenly looked very small to Jas, and more than a little frightened.

"She's right," said Lingiari, "in case we don't get out of this, and even if we do, one of us should stay out of it. Someone has to send a packet to Earth to tell them what's happening. We have to try to break through the security."

It was another thing Jas hadn't thought of. Everything was piling up on her. "Yeah. Lee, go and try to get into the comm system. We can buy you some time to get around Loba's security blackout. If you can, send a packet to Polestar and tell them everything that's happened. What am I talking about? Tell the Global Government. They have to know, or else the *Galathea* could turn up and infect the whole planet."

"Right," said Lee with undisguised relief. "Good luck," she called over her shoulder as she moved in the direction they'd come from.

"And hide," shouted Jas, after a moment's thought. "Pretend you're a techie...or something." But the navigator was gone. She didn't know if Lee had heard her.

27

Hauling the struggling Loba to the bridge was hard, even with Harrington's help. Carl had always admired her strength and fitness, and now he appreciated them even more. The master was heavier than he looked, and fought to free himself so strongly that Carl suspected he knew the other aliens wouldn't do a thing to save him. The master was also shouting, but his gag muffled the words.

As they got close to the bridge, they passed signs of a viciously fought battle. The walls, ceiling and floor were melted, pitted and scarred, and the infrastructure of the ship showed through. A horrible stench hung in the air.

"Ready?" asked Harrington, her expression pained.

"As I'll ever be," Carl replied. He grunted as they dragged the master over the holes and beams that were all that remained of the corridor floor. His feet trailed, bumping against metal ridges. They were nearly there. Had the infected officers heard Harrington's warning? Would they pay any attention? If he and the security officer were going to die, it was now.

Five possessed officers were blocking the corridor. They eyed the two of them and the bound and gagged Loba.

"Stand up," said Harrington, pushing the muzzle of her weapon roughly into the master's temple. His eyes hooded, the man grudgingly supported his own weight and stood. He averted his head from the watching officers.

"We know he's one of you," said Harrington. When none of the officers answered, she added, "And if we kill him, the one of you that's inside him will die."

Still the master and officers were silent. "You're thinking we won't kill him because he's the ship's master, right?" Carl asked. "You're wrong. The man's an arsehole, and we don't give a shit." He pointed his gun at Loba's foot and fired. The man screamed and fell to his knees, grabbing his wounded foot. Blood seeped through his fingers.

"Gee, Lingiari," whispered Harrington.

"Start talking," said Carl, "or I'll shoot higher."

"What do you want?" asked an officer. The words sounded a little strange, poorly formed, as if the man wasn't used to speaking.

"Let us on the bridge, now, or he dies." Harrington grabbed Loba's arm and hauled him, whimpering, to his feet. The master favored his uninjured foot and leaned against Carl.

The officers didn't reply or move. Carl wondered if they were speaking telepathically. Loba hung his head and closed his eyes. Was he begging for his life?

Carl sneaked a glance at Harrington. Her profile was set, fearless. He suddenly wished he'd had a chance to get to know her better. There had to be another side to this tough, cranky woman. He hoped they would get through this.

Still no one said anything. What if the stalemate continued? They didn't have a plan for this scenario. Harrington shot him a look, but he couldn't read her expression.

At last, the officers broke. "Give him to us," one said, "and we will allow you to enter the bridge."

These aliens had a low opinion of human intelligence. "We're not stupid," said Carl, and he aimed his gun at the master's other foot. Loba tried to move it out of Carl's sight, but this meant he had to put his weight onto his injured foot, and he partially collapsed.

"Time's up," said Harrington, and moved her finger to her weapon's trigger. Loba's eyes became wide. He yelled through his gag and wriggled violently. Carl had to dig his fingers into the man's bicep to maintain his grip.

"We will allow you onto the bridge," said the officer. "You do not need to give us your master." The other officers stepped away, clearing the path along the corridor. Their weapons dropped to their sides.

"Stay back," said Harrington. She pulled Loba forward, and Carl helped her drag the man through the waiting officers. He turned and pointed his weapon behind them as they passed, while Harrington kept hers trained on Loba's head.

"Think they'll let us in?" Carl asked the security officer softly.

"We'll soon find out."

The aliens must have been communicating telepathically, because the bridge door opened as they approached. The large room was empty but for one man. Grantwise, or rather, alien-infested Grantwise, sat at the ship's controls. The visual screen was up, and the planet surface was zooming up, the horizon flattening even as they watched. He was already taking the ship down.

"Krat." Dropping Loba, Carl ran to the intercom and

thumped the button with the flat of his hand. An alarm blared out, and the ship's lights began to flash. "Crew to crash seats, now," he shouted into the intercom. "This isn't a drill. This is not a drill. Crash seats immediately. Everyone."

Harrington had dragged Loba to the flight controls. She was trying to pull the pilot out of his seat while not losing her grip on the master. She couldn't do it. Loba wrenched himself out of her grasp and tried to escape, but as soon as he put his weight on his injured foot, he collapsed. He got to his feet, but Carl ran at him. He threw his shoulder into Loba, sending the master flying. Carl was on him. The two men grappled.

Infested officers poured into the room. Carl tried to bring his weapon round to fire at them, but Loba punched him in the head, and his shots went wide. The master landed another punch, spinning Carl around and knocking him nearly senseless. Everything seemed to slow down. As he turned, he saw Harrington struggling with Grantwise. She lifted her gun to his head. She was going to kill him. *Krat.* Then there wouldn't be anyone at the controls. What was she thinking?

Carl felt like he was floating. That was some punch Loba packed. Then Carl realized he really *was* floating. He was hanging in midair, halfway to the ceiling. Everyone was floating. The officers were spinning lazily, their hair trailing. Even Grantwise was lifting out of his seat. Harrington's expression was so surprised, Carl almost laughed.

What must have happened came to Carl in a flash. Confused by the increasing pull of the planet's gravity, the *Galathea's* gravity drive had cut out. But the ship was falling so fast their descent was matching the attraction of the planet's mass, canceling out the force's effect. Falling. They were dropping like a stone. The ship wasn't flying through the atmosphere, cruising to land. Whatever the hell Grantwise had done, the ship was out of control and they were going to crash.

Harrington hooked her feet under the flight control desk. She grabbed the pilot by the scruff of his neck, pulled him out of his seat and pushed him away.

Carl tried to move toward the controls, but ended up swimming comically in the air, not making any progress. He needed something to push against. Craning behind him, he saw Loba, who was grabbing for a weapon that was floating just out of his reach. Droplets of blood were gliding from his foot wound.

Two birds with one stone. Carl gave the master a mighty shove with his feet, sending the man spiralling out of the vicinity of the gun and himself closer to the flight controls. Harrington gripped the control desk with both hands and swung her body round so that her feet were toward him. No need for an explanation. He reached for her ankle and hauled himself hand over hand along her body until he was in reach of the desk.

A deep, searing pain ran up his leg. A shot had grazed his thigh. *Drongos.* If they didn't let him try to land the ship, they would all die. A series of hums sounded beside him as Harrington returned fire. He folded himself into the seat and slotted his legs under the desk. After putting his arms through the harness, he snapped the buckles closed. He was still floating a few centimeters above his seat, but he could concentrate on his task.

The horizon was a flat line. The next minute would be a killer.

28

Jas had one job: protect Lingiari. The loss of gravity had taken everyone by surprise, but now Loba and the officers were becoming accustomed to the weightlessness. Though she'd shoved him away as hard as she could, Grantwise was still the nearest of them. He floated only a couple of meters away from the flight control desk. Jas pointed her weapon at him. The man stopped reaching to get a grip on something, but from the corner of her eye she saw the other officers were taking advantage of her focus on the pilot. They were edging closer. She swung her weapon round.

One of her feet was hooked through the back of the pilot's seat, where Lingiari floated against the straps of his safety harness. He was furiously swiping the pilot's interface, bringing up fast-flowing figures. He began keying in numbers and dragging his fingers across the screen, altering levels. The visual on the planet surface told her there was only the remotest chance they would make it.

A shadow to her left. Grantwise had managed to lock a finger on the pilot's seat. Without even thinking about it, she fired at the hand, severing it at the wrist. The pilot floated away, blood flowing from his stump, a look of disbelief on his face. His hand remained hooked by its pinky finger on the seat. The pilot's blood had sprayed the back of Lingiari's neck, but he didn't seem to notice.

"Come on," he muttered, glancing at the visual. "Come on, girl."

Jas swept the remaining officers with her gun. Grantwise's experience had dampened their enthusiasm about attacking. Or maybe they'd realized that the copilot was their only chance of survival. Everyone needed him to succeed now. The officers hung in the air, watching.

"What's happening, Lingiari?"

"Working on it."

"Have we had it?"

The copilot didn't answer. They were going to die. There was no way Lingiari could pull the starship out of its dive. It was impossible. This was it.

Jas gazed at the alien-infested officers. She wondered what they were saying to each other in their heads. Were they wishing they'd done things differently? Did they regret inhabiting the foreign species that had come to their planet?

Did she have any regrets? She'd always thought things might end something like this, given the nature of her job. At least the loss of her life wouldn't break anyone's heart. She had no parents or siblings who would never see her again, no child who would lose its mother. Was there anything she would have done differently? She recalled Lee's comment about her temper. Maybe the woman had a point. Maybe if she hadn't gotten angry that day in the mission room, if she'd taken the time to talk to the other officers privately and gotten their support, none of this would have happened. If she'd done things differently,

Margret, Loba, and the rest of the officers might not have got possessed. Or Haggardy. What had happened to him? She hadn't figured that out.

Maybe this was all her fault.

A hand gripped her calf. Reflexively, she pointed her gun down, only to realize the hand belonged to Lingiari.

"I've done all I can." He was shouting, though the bridge of the *Galathea* was eerily quiet. It was strange how they could be traveling so fast yet so silently.

"We're gonna crash," Lingiari said. He was pulling her down into the copilot's seat. In the visual ahead, the scrubby landscape of K. 67092d flew up dizzyingly fast.

"I've leveled her off the best I can. Full reverse thrust." Lingiari was still shouting for some reason.

Jas was fumbling with the buckles of her harness. "Can starships—" she said as they hit.

29

Carl could never remember much of what happened when the *Galathea* crashed on K. 67092d. The hull of the deep space vessel protected those inside from the sound of it sweeping through kilometers of soil, rocks, and vegetation, cutting a swathe along the planet's surface. He vaguely recalled the flight control visual showing the landscape flowing past like a runaway express train before the connection was destroyed and the screen went blank. After that, there was only the terrible juddering that made him feel as though his teeth were being shaken out of his head and his bones shattered.

With more than a hundred meters of engine lying between them and the ground, Carl dreaded to think what the juddering meant in terms of the prospect of the engines ever working again and allowing them to leave the planet.

Grantwise, Loba, and the other infected officers had dropped to the floor like stones when the *Galathea* had hit, and the one point two Earth gravity of the planet had become suddenly and terribly present. Carl kept his gaze averted from them while the ship was grinding to a halt. There was nothing he could do anyway.

After what seemed like forever, the shaking stopped. Carl realized his eyes were closed. He opened them. The main lights were out. Emergency lighting had come on, making the bridge look like something from a low-grade horror movie. Only the monsters looked human, and they were lying in contorted positions around the deck, not moving.

He hardly dared to look toward the copilot's seat, but after a moment's hesitation, he stole a glance. He exhaled. Harrington was alive, though her expression was drawn and, if it weren't for the dull red lighting, he was sure she would be as white as a ghost. She returned his look and seemed glad that he'd made it too. She gave him a weak smile. In his memory, it was the first time he'd ever seen her do that. He liked the effect.

"Good job, Lingiari," the security officer said.

"How're you doing? Break anything?"

Harrington unclipped her harness and moved her arm and legs, rotating her wrists and ankles. "I think I'm okay. How about you?"

"Still alive, so no complaints." He risked another look at the bodies around them. "Can't say the same for those poor buggers."

Grantwise must have been head down when the *Galathea* had impacted the planet surface. Blood mixed with brain matter oozed from his shattered skull. Loba was on his back, his eyes open and blank, his mouth gaping and bloody. Half a severed tongue lay next to him. The rest of the officers were also visibly, graphically dead.

Vomit forced its way into Carl's mouth, and he turned his head to let it out. When his stomach was finally empty and he could retch no more, he collapsed back into his seat and closed his eyes. The rustle of clothing to his side told him Harrington was getting up. He should, too. They had to check on the crew and find out who needed their help. He unclipped his harness and pulled himself to his feet. He took another look at Grantwise. He'd always envied the man. His job, his status, his distinction, and popularity were all that Carl had wanted. It was funny that now that *he* was the pilot, the only pilot on board, he found he didn't care anymore. And he was sure Grantwise would have given it all up to be able to live.

The shuttle was gone and the *Galathea* was unlikely to fly again. Now, their lives would be a matter of survival until they could be rescued. Status, distinction and popularity—none of them would count for anything.

Harrington was already at the ship's comm center. Carl joined her. She was pressing the panel, but it stayed dark. She spoke into the mic. "Ship's crew, ship's crew?" No sound of her words came from the corridor outside. The comm system was down. "Looks like we're operating on face-to-face comm," she said.

"Figures," said Carl. "That was some crash landing. We'll have to see what else it took out. Let's have a look around."

They went first to the medical center. There would be injuries, no doubt, and they needed to know how well Sparks was set up to deal with them, assuming he'd survived.

The door was closed but not locked. They slid it open, pushing it into its recess. Dr. Sparks had obeyed Carl's instruction to get into his crash seat, and he hadn't left it. The man was trembling, and the whites of his eyes showed. It was only after repeated assurances that he was safe that he undid his harness and rose from the seat. Harrington told him to check his equipment and find out what was still working. She also told him to ready his first aid supplies, because they would no doubt be sending him some casualties soon.

The man said barely a word in reply. As they left him, he was counting the same bandages over and over again.

A few people wandered the corridors, dazed. The crew members were beginning to venture from their cabins. Sounds of groaning and crying were coming from some rooms. Carl and Harrington located the injured personnel to see what they could do to help. Most of the traumas the crew had suffered weren't severe. The copilot and security officer matched up healthy crew with those in need of medical treatment, and instructed them to take the injured along to Sparks and give him what support they could. Some of the crew were on this already.

They came across several dead infected officers, including Margret and the second mate, whom Alef had shot. They were in the personal cabin area, checking each room. Carl was pondering how they were going to get down the side of the ship to the planet surface, and if they even *wanted* to get to the planet surface, when a thought struck him with horror. He hadn't seen Flux. He didn't know if the little fella had survived the crash.

He dashed into a cabin. It was empty. Leaping onto a chair, he pulled the covering off an air vent and shouted his friend's name into the aperture.

"I forgot about your pet," said Harrington.

"He's not a pet," replied Carl before shouting the name again. He waited. No familiar rustling of wings was coming from the shaft. He waited some more. Carl stepped down from the chair and ran a hand through his hair. Where might Flux have gone? Had he heard Carl's warning? Had he been able to get somewhere safe before the ship had crashed?

"Try not to worry," said Harrington. "He seemed pretty tough to me. Come on. I'll help you find him."

"Thanks, but I dunno where to look. He can fit in places people can't. He could be anywhere."

"Well, where's his favorite place? Maybe he went there."

Carl frowned, then his face brightened. "I know." He ran from the cabin, and arrived at his own room in record time. Though it was his own, it looked unfamiliar. He could hardly believe he'd last been in it less than a day ago. "Flux?" he called into empty air. There was no answer. *Krat.* He noticed the covers on his bunk were lumpy. One of the lumps was Flux-sized. Could it be him? Under Carl's covers was the animal's favorite place to sleep. If it was him, why wasn't he answering?

"Could you..." he said to Harrington, pointing at the bunk, "could you check there for me?"

The security officer went over and gently lifted the Polestar blanket. The pale brown creature was lying in the middle of the bunk, wrapped in his wings, taking up the best spot, as was his habit. His eyes were closed. A wave of despair welled up in Carl's chest. He put a hand over his face and turned away.

"Hold on, I think he's asleep," said Harrington. "Look, he's breathing."

Carl leapt to the bunk and gently picked up the animal. His wings unfolded, and his eyes opened. He gave a great yawn. "Flux, you..." Carl cursed at his buddy.

"Woah, calm down you...," Flux swore at Carl in return. "I was only taking a nap." He climbed onto Carl's shoulder and began grooming himself.

Harrington also swore. "Lingiari, there's someone else we're forgetting. Where's Lee?"

Carl's eyes widened. "You're right. Where would she be? Where haven't we looked?"

"I told her to send Earth a packet. She could do that from any comm access point, but she would have been trying to hide from the infected officers. I don't think she would have gone to her own cabin."

"I know. Maybe she went back to our rendezvous point," said Carl.

The two of them ran to Margret's cabin. Carl's guess had been correct. The navigator was there. But she was on the floor by Margret's bunk. In her concern to send a message packet to Earth, she hadn't sat in the cabin's crash seat in time. She was on her back. Her eyes were closed, and her face was peaceful. She looked as though she were sleeping, but when Harrington listened to her chest, she couldn't hear a heartbeat.

30

The ship was falling. Things were going badly wrong. It was ever thus on the physical plain. The same problem plagued them once they left the void. Now that they were inhabiting individual bodies, they could no longer meld and flow into and through each other, and they began to differ.

The alien had not been identified by the humans, and it needed to remain hidden. Soon, it might be the only one of its kind left aboard the starship. The one who had replaced the commander of the space vessel had failed. It had made errors of judgment, underestimating the resourcefulness of the humans called Harrington, Lingiari, and Lee, and allowing them to take control of the equipment items used for attack and defense. It was also due to the failed one's incompetency that the humans had destroyed the shuttle-craft, the best method of transportation to the planetary traps.

Error upon error compiled. The commander replacement deserved to die, yet it had begged for its life. Foolish. Already, it had lost its understanding that they were all one.

Its ending did not matter if they succeeded in their aim. One life signified nothing. And the others...the others had agreed to save it! They had identified their own individuality within the threatened one. They had empathized. Madness.

Its arguments had gone unheard. The others had decided to risk everything to save one, an insignificance, as they all were when compared to the whole.

Before they left the void, the steps were laid out clearly: replication, generation, domination. Nothing else mattered. Its kind were not like the species of the physical realm. It pitied their separation. It did not wish to become like them. The others had adopted this insanity, but it would not. It would hold true to the plan.

Its advantage was that it had not acted with the others. The humans did not know it for what it was. For the time being, it could safely move among them, unrecognized. If the others did not succeed—and according to the thoughts it could read as they fought the humans at the ship's controls, it looked as though they would not—it could continue to work toward its goal, undiscovered.

If the others were destroyed, it would survive as the last replicant. Only one was needed to move onto the next step. Let the humans kill its fellows. Seduced by the egoism of individuality, they were useless already. They did not deserve to return to the void and reunite. They would bring only contamination and perversion.

Only let it survive this terrible fall to the entrapment planet, and it would hold true to the goal of its kind. They would dominate this solid world. They would control all its inhabitants and bend them to their will. They would have everything they wanted. All they needed was another world on which to open their traps. These humans were wise to their ways, but on a new planet, they would find fresh bodies to absorb and replicate.

It must stay silent and safe, and all would be well in time.

A voice came over the intercom: "Crew to crash seats, now. This isn't a drill. This is not a drill. Crash seats immediately. Everyone."

It slipped into a seat in the cabin and fastened its safety belt.

31

"Grab her legs," said Jas, lifting the navigator's shoulders.

"But, I thought she's..." said Lingiari.

"She's not dead," shouted Jas. "She's not dead until she's warm and dead. Let's see if that misborn doctor can do his job."

The copilot's features clouded. "I get what you mean, but do really think she'd want that? Here? When there's no hope...?"

"I'm not asking you, Lingiari. It's an order. Help me carry her or damn me but I'll drag her there by myself."

The copilot lifted the limp Lee's legs, and the two of them ran with her, carrying the navigator between them like a hunting kill.

At the medical center, Sparks was surrounded by injured crew and uninjured crew members who were trying to help him. The place was in chaos. It was a chaos that Jas cleared with a bellowed order for everyone to get out of their way. The crowd cleaved, creating a path to the beleaguered doctor, who was talking to a patient with a bloody, gashed knee who was sitting on his examining couch. The patient hobbled out of the way at the sight of Jas and Lingiari carrying the fatally hurt navigator. They laid her down gently.

The doctor stiffened at the sight of Jas, and quickly hunched over Lee. He held a stethoscope to her heart, shone a torch into her eyes, and rubbed his knuckles against her chest. Jas watched like a hawk. When his brief examination was complete, Sparks looked at the floor and shook his head.

"No. We can put her in stasis," said Jas.

"I'm afraid it's too late for that," replied the doctor. "She's been oxygen-deprived for too long. I could operate, but her brain has been irreparably damaged."

"No, it isn't too late. People who have been dead longer than her have been brought back. Put her on life support, now, and we'll start up the stasis bank."

"But—"

Jas leaned toward the doctor until their noses almost touched. "Life support. Now," she breathed.

As if touched by a cattle prod, Sparks leapt into action, calling for help to move Lee.

The security officer and Lingiari went next door to the stasis room. Like the rest of the ship, only emergency lighting illuminated it. Jas went immediately to one of four small, square doors set in the metal wall and pressed the screen next to it. It remained black.

"Harrington," said Lingiari. Jas ignored him and tried another panel, which also failed to light up. "Harrington." She tried a third panel with the same result. "H—"

"WHAT?" Jas turned on the copilot, rage threatening to overwhelm her.

The man shook his head. "Never mind."

Jas breathed deeply in and out. "Sorry. I'm sorry I shouted. I overreacted. I'm trying to get a handle on that. What did you want to say?"

"The stasis containers aren't working because we're on emergency power. Preserving what's left of the dead isn't a priority on a stricken ship. I'm sorry, Harrington, but Lee's had it."

Jas gazed into the man's eyes as she tried to comprehend what he was saying. He was right, but his words didn't fit with what she wanted to hear, with what she needed to hear. Though the last twenty-four hours had been harrowing, she felt like she'd developed a bond with this man and with the woman lying all but dead in the medical center, a bond that was closer than she'd ever been to another human being but one.

For a moment, for a split second, Jas nearly let down the adamantine facade she'd built up to protect herself from the vulnerability of human companionship. She nearly fell into Lingiari's arms and sobbed. Then the moment was gone. She wasn't prepared to lose anyone ever again. She would not let that happen. "The units," she exclaimed. "The defense units. We can use their power to keep Lee in stasis."

The copilot's eyes widened. "Do you think?"

"We have to try, Lingiari. Come on."

LOCATING the defense units took longer than Jas liked, and several of them—the ones who had tried to force entry to the bridge—were still too damaged to be of any use, but eventually they had four of the remaining ones jerry-rigged up to the stasis unit.

Jas and Lingiari watched as Sparks placed Lee in the

stasis container. A couple of hours on life support had lent the navigator a deceptively healthy color, and it was difficult to believe, watching her chest rise and fall as the machine breathed for her, that she was essentially dead. Jas's hope was that enough of her mind had survived, and that, when they finally made it back to Earth, even if the rest of her brain was useless, the cloners could grow her another body in which to transfer the personality, experiences, and memories that comprised Navigator Lee.

There might have been some murmurs of resentment among the crew that the defense units, their most valuable assets, were being devoted to the probably hopeless endeavor to preserve the mind of a single crew member, but Jas chose not to hear them. And so far, no one had stepped forward to question her authority.

Several hours later, a thorough survey of the ship had revealed many facts. Fresh water still flowed through the pipes, though no one knew for how long, and there was no air movement from the vents, not even a breath. This meant that the ship's air wasn't being recycled, filtered, or replenished with oxygen. Though it would take weeks for the loss to be noticeable, if they couldn't fix the system, they would eventually have to open up the ship to allow the planet's atmosphere inside. Without air being warmed, the temperatures aboard ship would align with the local levels, which were uncomfortably low. They lacked waste recycling, too, and without that they would be relying on the finite supply of food in the hold. There'd been no indication there was anything fit for human consumption on the planet.

In short, they couldn't survive being stranded there forever.

JAS WAS LYING on her bunk in her cabin, beyond exhausted and trying to sleep, when there was a knock at the door. She wearily got to her feet and pushed it open. What she saw snapped her awake. Two of the crew had brought Haggardy to her. First Mate Haggardy, technically now the master of the ship.

"Bring him in," she said, returning to her bunk.

She'd almost forgotten about the man. Nearly every crew member of the *Galathea* had been accounted for. The infected officers they knew of were all dead, though there was a question over exactly who else might have been infected. The rest of the crew had survived without life-threatening casualties.

And then there was Haggardy.

"I know what you're thinking," said the first mate.

"You do, do you?" Jas leaned back on her arms. "What's that?"

"It's no secret I went down to the planet. I was forced to, like the others, but I wasn't affected like the rest. I was never possessed by aliens. I outwitted Loba, and pretended to be one of them. I had nothing to do with what they did. I didn't hurt anybody."

Jas recalled that Haggardy had been there when they destroyed the shuttle, and that he hadn't countermanded her when he'd had the opportunity, but she wasn't going to help him out with that tidbit.

"I don't know, Haggardy. Why should I believe you? I have no way of telling who you are. The simplest solution would be to force you off the ship."

"Don't do that," he blurted, glancing behind him at the two crew members who hovered in Jas's doorway. "I tell you what, I promise I'll defer to your command. Now that Loba's dead, I'm next in rank, and I should assume leadership. But

I won't. I'll stand aside, and I'll tell the crew that. You can be master of the ship."

"Me? Master?" Jas hadn't thought about who should lead them now. "But shouldn't it be...?" She paused and tried to remember who was above her in the chain of command.

"They're all dead, Harrington. Second and third mate, chief engineer, purser, and I hear you've put Lee in stasis. Below me, there's no one left until we get to you."

The enormity of what the man was suggesting grew in Jas's mind. She'd felt like her job was done. Together, she, Lingiari and Lee had defeated the aliens in their attempt to take over the ship.

But now someone had to coordinate the survival effort, lead the crew, and keep them safe from the aliens that still threatened them. While they waited for rescue, someone had to maintain morale. Could she do it?

She regarded the first mate. One thing was for sure—she couldn't trust this man.

"Take him to the brig."

As Haggardy was led away, Jas lay down. She was exhausted. Tomorrow, she would think about what to do next, but for now, she would sleep.

JAS'S STORY CONTINUES IN
STRANDED

SHADOWS OF THE VOID BOOK 2